Surrendering the Reins

Written by Les Graham

Copyright © 2015 by Les Graham

ISBN #978-0-9904775-2-5

Library of Congress Control Number: 2015904682

Published by:
BRITCHIN BOOKS by Colfax Publishing
616 270th Ave NW Suite G
New London, MN 56273

Printed by:
Lakeside Press
PO Box 1075
Willmar, MN 56201 USA
(320) 235-5849

Table of Contents

Acknowledgements

First and foremost, I want to thank all the readers of *Jude's Gentle Giants*. Without ALL their positive feedback and support, the second book never would have happened! My wife Kathy and my children; Kale, Ben and Rebecca. They were there for front cover shoots, videos, manuscript reads, etc.... I get tunnel vision at times and they keep me on the right track.

My first editor, April Kummrow, added many thoughtful suggestions. She was very thorough and professional. Thank you April!

Tia Johnson, an author herself, did the second edit. She was gracious enough to take time in her VERY busy schedule. Her insight was greatly appreciated and timely.

Mark and Marie Peterson were the final editors, as they were for *Jude's Gentle Giants*. They kept this project on schedule. I thank them for keeping their cool when working with a novice on a book project.

Lakeside Press designed the awesome cover and the layout of the inside of the book. Their team was easy to work with and treated the project like it was their own. Thank you for your professionalism!

Mike Bregel, the illustrator, again proved his ability with his GREAT illustrations. It has been an honor to get to know him better, even though he beats me in ice hockey most Thursday nights. His illustrations add so much to the book. Thank you, Mike!

God is HOLY! I thank God for allowing me to come closer to Him during these endeavors. I have been blessed!

May God Bless,
Les Graham

Endorsements

"*Surrendering the Reins* is a fine sequel to Les Graham's *Jude's Gentle Giants*. The author knows young people, horses, and the God he serves. We continue to follow Jude Bonner as he faces and makes some of the most significant decisions of his life. The narrative reminds us that the life of the Christian is not a journey that is free of pain and disappointment. Sometimes, as the prophet Jeremiah reminds us, we have to 'run with horses' (Jer.12:5). I encourage you to read this book and meet a God who will help you run the race!"

Jim Fretheim

"*Pete and Joe certainly stole the show in* Jude's Gentle Giants. *In author Les Graham's well-crafted sequel,* Surrendering the Reins, *the unconditional love and undying devotion to their master, Jude Bonner, of this magnificent pair of Persherons is a reminder to Jude Bonner and to all of us the perfect love God has for His loyal servants.*"

Bill Dean, host of *The Morning Brew* talk show on KWLM Radio, Willmar, Minnesota

"*Les Graham takes true-to-life scenarios and culminates them into a finale without missing a beat. The narrative is a possibility of how young Christian men should handle the complex problems of life. His books could easily be incorporated into the literature component of Christian education.*"

Samuel W. Greene
Christian Educator/Author

"*Les Graham's humor and knowledge of horses is masterfully woven into this country-Minnesotan novel. It won't disappoint you.*"

Tia Johnson
Author

Chapter 1

"Who Gets Revenge"

Yes, in more ways than one Greg Shants was right, I would remember that prom night. Not only did I go to prom with a girl I used to despise, but Pete and Joe, my very own Percheron geldings, drove us there. And last but not least, Greg Shants and his boys punched my lights out.

I woke the next morning with my stomach killing me. It hurt to breathe, bend over, and walk. I thought I was going to die as I pitched some manure. You never think about your stomach muscles until they are screaming for relief from every little thing you do. Chores took longer than normal that morning as I moved like an 80-year old. With each shot of pain, I found my anger building toward Greg Shants.

I was having a hard time with God for allowing Greg and his boys to have their way with me. I found myself scheming to get even, which of course involved me pounding on them in several different scenarios. As always, just like in the movies, I was untouched by the bad guys as they lay there wishing they were never born. I leaned over the pitch fork in a trance as I pictured myself standing over them, victorious.

"Jude, are you alright?" Dad asked, startling me out of my trance.

I tried to stand upright without Dad seeing I was hurting. "Yeah, I'm fine. I guess I was just daydreaming."

"Son, I thought I would never have to ask you this. Are you hung over?"

I started to laugh, but that only made my stomach muscles hurt all the more. I bent over in pain as I couldn't stop laughing. I'm sure Dad was wondering how I could laugh about his question. I slowly straightened up with the help of the fork handle and looked Dad in the eye.

"Dad, I'm sorry. No I'm not hung over, but Greg and his boys beat the snot out of me last night. My stomach muscles are killing me this morning. You caught me thinking of how I was going to get even."

"Is that all that's wrong?" Dad laughed a little. "Why, I was worried there for a second."

"Is that all! You make it sound like those jerks beating the crap out of me is okay! Whose side are you on?" I complained to Dad.

Dad scratched his forehead as he thought. "I'm on God's side. You know what the Bible says about pride and how it comes before a fall." Dad walked away and left me standing there dumbfounded. How could Dad blame me? What did I do wrong? What pride do I have? All these questions came to mind as I followed Dad in for breakfast. With each step my anger grew. I slammed the back door as I stepped into the utility room.

"Dad, we need to talk!" I demanded. "How can you stand there and tell me this is my fault?!"

"Jude, you've grown up to be a fine young man. You've had a lot of help from Mr. Olson, Carl Toney, your mother, Becky, Fuzz, Pete and Joe, and mostly God our Father. If you think about it, Judy even changed your life a lot. Your life has been fairly smooth compared to many. So, God gives you a bump in the road with some kid named Greg Shants, and you want to make a mountain out of it. Do you really think you're so special that you're supposed go through life with no hiccups? The Bible talks of doing all things without complaining." Dad walked into the kitchen.

I stood there speechless. Was Dad right? Did I think I was special? Did I think I was better than others? Did I ever think how nice my life really was compared to many? My mind was going in all directions. I slowly walked to the kitchen scratching my head.

"Jude, after breakfast you need to use the concordance in the back of your bible and look up pride, revenge and forgiveness. Talk with God as you look up all the verses related to those words. Let God tell you where you're at." He started laughing softly while stirring his coffee. "Oh how I remember when I got my bell rung back in third grade by Sam Turnquist. I came home looking for sympathy from my mother, thinking she would fix everything. She gave me a little hug, looked me in the eye, and said I would be fine. Jude, you're putting a lot of energy into this fight you had and rightly so, but this is how God builds you and teaches you. Someday you'll look back on this and chuckle at how small it is compared to other mountains God wants you to climb."

"But Dad, it was three against one!"

"Jude, read those Bible verses and pray about it! Romans 12:19 talks about not seeking revenge and allowing God's wrath to work. Satan is telling you to get revenge; God is telling you He will do it. Who are you going to listen to? Now, if I was a young man in this situation. I would be doing pull-ups, push-ups and building some strength just in case God uses you to bring His wrath to Mr. Greg Shants."

Chapter 2

"Graduation Day and Life"

For seniors, the next big event after prom was graduation.
I was looking forward to graduation day, but I wasn't looking
forward to all the work Mom wanted done around the farm for
the party. Dad always teased her that it would be simpler to just
bulldoze everything and start over. Becky and Mom planted a
bunch of different flowers. Dad and I had to add shutters to the
house and do some landscape work around our back patio. We
hauled picnic tables over from all the neighbors. Mom recruited a
couple of her sisters to help serve food for the day of the party.

Graduation day was upon us and we were lucky the weather
was great. Perry was valedictorian of the class. Harold was asked
to sing a solo, which I thought was great. He chose to sing "God
Bless America." Mom cried her eyes out. Her little boy was
starting to move on. Judy had written a poem about school days in
Belgrade High School and was asked to read it. She did a fine job
and even mentioned God's transforming ways in her life. Again,
Mom cried.

My graduation party was perfect. All my uncles and aunts
came by. We had volleyball, horseshoes, and badminton going.
Fuzz was beside herself with all these people to keep track of.
Mom was able to mingle with everyone instead of being tied to
the kitchen. Judy came by with her parents, which surprised us
all. After I mingled with all my guests I quietly slipped over to
the volleyball court. Tom, one of my first cousins, was standing

to the side watching the people play. Tom was like ten years older than I and served our country with the Army in Afghanistan. I really didn't know him that well because of the age difference and all the tours he had done. Dad said the war had changed him and that he was concerned for him. I wondered if I could talk him into a good game of volleyball.

"Tom thanks for coming over today for my special day."

He looked my way but wouldn't make eye contact. "No problem, thanks for inviting me." He shuffled his feet back and forth.

I looked towards the volleyball court and asked. "How about you get on one side and I get on the other side and we'll see if I can get schooled after just graduating."

I looked back to Tom and he had a slight grin on his face. I think he was taking my bait.

"Jude, I don't know."

"Come on, I'd consider it an honor to play a game or two." I walked toward the court.

There were about three kids on each side hitting the ball back and forth. I asked them if Tom and I could join in and much to my surprise Tom walked to the other side of the net. We started a makeshift game and wow was I amazed at Tom's skill level. He was all over that court. We were soon joined by Judy, Becky, Perry, and Harold.

The game was getting stronger the longer we played. The smaller kids kind of weeded themselves out. It was now Tom, Becky and Harold against Judy, Perry and myself. We started to draw a little bit of a crowd as the game intensified. Tom was in a zone, he was hammering that ball down our throats as Becky gave him perfect sets. Perry and I would try to double block him and he would just hit over us. I'd never seen someone play with such intensity yet play the game true to form. He was putting on a clinic without saying a word.

All of us were having a blast as we fought for each point. When we called it quits our team had lost three in a row with no wins.

As I walked off the court I said to Tom. "Next time I graduate from high school I won't ask you to play volleyball. Wow, that was fun!"

Tom shook my hand. "Jude, I gotta go. Thanks for the food and the game."

I walked Tom to his pick-up as he was wiping sweat from his brow. "Tom, thank you for serving our country. Ya know I owe you an apology, I never sent you any cards or letters while you were overseas. I really feel bad about that." He stood with his hand on the pick-up door handle. "It's okay Jude, don't worry about it." He shook my hand. "Congrats Jude, and thanks again for the game, I needed that."

As Tom drove out the drive I could hear the sound of loud exhaust pipes getting closer. "No way," I thought. It couldn't be Greg Shants. Sure enough, it was. He was gunning his engine and squealing his tires. He turned onto the gravel road and the dust flew into the air as he turned donuts on the loose gravel. I caught myself wanting to go out there and confront him, but that was what he wanted, so I chose to ignore him.

Summer hit with a flurry. I was working at the Army Surplus store and helping out at home, plus getting ready for college. I also wanted to train Pete and Joe to ride and maybe even drive Roman style. To top it off, I caught myself thinking of Judy a lot.

Becky and I were working with Pete and Joe for under saddle. Because of all the other training they had been through, they took to the saddles very well. Many times when I would get home from work, Becky would be riding one of them. I told Becky I wanted to get them going well enough for Judy and me to ride together some night.

It was sweet to be sitting up that high. Becky and I would ride over to Mr. Olson's and sometimes he would get on Molly and ride with us. We had pheasants flush right beside us! Wow, that was kind of neat. Pete and Joe would jump sideways about three feet in a half second, all two thousand pounds, and then settle right down. I would ride them to check gopher traps. Dad and I would ride together at times, and Dad seemed to really enjoy that.

It was now time to plan a ride with Judy. I wanted to make it special, so I planned to have a picnic lunch with her out on the trail. I sent Judy an invitation in the mail and asked for an e-mail back confirming the RSVP. I received an e-mail within a couple of days stating she could make it. The day of our first ride was a Saturday, and I did all my fixing of food the night before. The menu consisted of brats, potato chips, mixed fruit, brownies, and lemonade. The brats would be cooked over a little fire as we rested the horses. I made sure everything would fit in my backpack, including the ice pack to keep things cool. I had to work Saturday till two at the surplus store, then I hustled home, took a shower, got the food ready and headed to the barn. Judy was right on time. She pulled in as I was walking into the barn.

"Oh, Jude, I'm so excited to ride today, and it's perfect weather."

"Yes, ma'am, it sure is. Would you like to curry and saddle Pete or did you want me to?"

"I'd love to do it myself. That way Pete can start getting used to me."

I handed her a rope halter and we headed toward the pasture gate. When we got to the gate I asked her, "How about a friendly wager here?"

"Depends on what's involved."

"Well, the loser has to shovel poop out of the barn. In or out?"

"Sure, but I don't plan on losing," she said with confidence.

"Okay, I'm betting that Pete and Joe ignore your whistle, but they come to the gate when I whistle."

"You're on." Judy stood there and whistled loudly. The geldings were in the woods, so we couldn't see them. I listened for the sound of thundering hooves. Nope, nothing. She whistled again. Nothing.

"Give up yet?"

"One more try, please."

She took a deep breath and let out the longest whistle ever. We listened and heard some thundering hooves coming. Judy was all smiles and so was I because I knew what those hooves belonged to. Sure enough, it was the sows rounding the corner in the hog pasture. I couldn't help but bust out laughing. Judy looked bewildered as the sows stood there looking at her.

"Judy, it looks like you're gonna have to ride a pig today. It's an old, old family tradition around here that whatever you call in you've got to ride. Ya know it's very sinful to break a family tradition. You can curry and saddle any one of them sows while I whistle in Joe."

"Jude Bonner, don't give me that family tradition stuff."

I whistled and sure enough the ground started shaking. Pete and Joe were heading in right away. They ran up to the gate to meet us.

"Good boys, good boys! Now you guys poop all you want in the barn today and tell Judy that you only listen to my whistle."

As I slipped a rope halter on Joe, Judy watched every step. She headed right to Pete and repeated what I had done. I liked that! She took the initiative to do things without being told. We led the geldings into the barn and starting currying them. The sunlight peeked through a few cracks in the barn wall and you could see horse hair floating off their backs.

As she curried she bartered. "Pete, Joe, you just keep everything to yourselves till we get out of this barn."

"The scoop shovel is hanging on the south wall, Judy." I laughed.

It wasn't long before Pete emptied out some road apples. Judy looked at me, looked at Pete and headed for the shovel without saying a word. You could tell she hadn't used a scoop shovel before. It took her several trips to get all those apples. She had just hung up the shovel when Joe left his deposits on the floor.

"Thataboy, Joe, good job. Nice big pile. Good boy."

Judy headed for the shovel again. Trying not to smile, I repeated, "Shovel is on the south wall."

Judy got that pile cleaned up and it was time to throw saddles on. She carefully watched me throw on the blanket and the saddle. I stood back and watched her, first the blanket, then the saddle. Saddles are pretty heavy and Pete is pushing eighteen hands. She hoisted it above her head and vaulted it onto Pete's back. Not too bad for a beginner. I knew what was coming next but Judy didn't.

As usual, Pete and Joe emptied their large intestines in unison.

"Shovel is on the south wall. It's all in the whistle, right Pete and Joe."

Judy started toward the shovel while she looked back at me. Boom! She walked right into the barn post. That knocked her back a few steps and right into my arms. "Careful there Judy that post has been there a long time." I said as I held her.

"You just wait Jude, someday Pete and Joe will come to my whistle. And when they do it will be a very special day. Are you going to hold me all day or can I get the shovel?"

"Not sure, you're so light it really isn't much of a chore, but I suppose I better let you get to work."

"Good boys, good boys, I knew you could do it." I stood by their rumps as Judy cleaned up the piles. "Sure is a nice day today."

Judy diligently shoveled the alley clean, trying her best to ignore my comments. When she finished, she hung the shovel back up and came and stood by me.

As I looked her in the eye, I asked, "Are you ready to go, ma'am?"

She didn't answer at first and just stood there with the sweetest gleam in her eye. I stood there for a second, gazing back into her eyes of blue. We finally realized that we were eye locked on each other. It was a little awkward, and she cleared her throat as I started to explain what was next.

"We need to walk them some down the driveway. This allows us to get the cinch straps tighter because they let more air out of their chests as we walk. Then I'll give you a boost up, a little riding lesson and off we go."

It was neat to watch Judy as she rode. She seemed pretty proud of what she was doing. Pete was great and doing well for her. We stopped by Mr. Olson's to say a quick hello. He was just heading out to go to town so we didn't talk much.

"What do you think so far, Judy?"

She smiled a huge smile and said, "This is awesome. I never thought I'd like to ride a horse, but this is great! It is so peaceful and these guys are so majestic."

"Gentle giants."

She smiled and said, "Jude's gentle giants."

We got about a mile and a half from home and Judy started laughing a little. I looked her way and she tried to suppress it, but soon she had started in again. What was going on?

"Okay, tell me, what's so funny?"

She laughed all the harder as she said, "Do you remember riding your bike here and, ah, Greg and I drove past and splashed all that cold water on you? I looked back just as you were falling in the water." She could hardly finish what she was saying, she was laughing so hard. I tried not to, but the more she laughed the more I laughed. I had to admit, thinking back about it now, it did seem pretty funny.

"Yes, ma'am that was something I will never forget! That water was ice cold and stinky. I had to ride all the way home soaking wet. By the time I got home my clothes were frozen and so stiff I could barely get out of them."

"I hope, ah, I hope you took a picture for one of those family traditions!" She was laughing like crazy by now. Pete even stopped as she hung over the saddle horn trying not to fall off.

She blurted out, "You might say we baptized you that day."

Judy was wiping tears away and so was I as we got the horses going again. We pulled into our picnic spot and tied the geldings up to a couple of oak saplings. Judy helped me with the back pack, we gathered some small sticks and we soon had a small fire going. I whittled a couple of roasting sticks for the brats while Judy set up the plates and lemonade.

As we ate, we talked about her faith walk and how her parents were doing. She explained that both her parents were alcoholics and thought she was crazy to go to church. They weren't very happy about her hanging around with me and warned her not to trust me.

I asked her, "What do you tell them when you come over to our place, then?"

"I just tell them how my life has changed ever since coming to Christ and that I've never been happier or had so much joy. I've tried to tell them about Jesus but they want none of it. As far as hanging out with you, I just read in Exodus in the Bible about honoring your parents. I think it's best if you came over someday for supper so they could get to know you better."

I stopped and thought about going to Judy's house. I had to admit it wasn't real high on my list.

I then asked Judy. "Do you know what a generational sin is?"

Judy thought for a moment. "No."

"It's very common that kids do the same sin as their parents. Dad talks about his bad habits so I can try not to follow them. Even though you dislike that your parents drink a lot, you have a very good chance of doing the same thing. I would talk with Pastor Carl about generational sins and how to deal with them."

"Jude."

"Yes?"

"After prom, when you dropped me off, I thought we might give each other a quick kiss. If I offended you, I'm sorry. Was I wrong for expecting a simple kiss?"

"Hey, I'm glad you brought that up. You need to understand that I believe in courting instead of dating."

"Courting?"

"Courting, in my opinion, is spending time with someone of the opposite sex three or four times and then asking myself if I want to marry that girl someday. If the answer is no, then I will not continue that relationship as a serious courting type deal. I will be friends with that girl only. Dating is not biblical because

Surrendering the Reins 17

of sin and all the stupid things a guy can do because of his hormones. I probably should have said something to you sooner. I consider this our second courting time."

"Jude, it seems weird that we're on our second date and you are mentioning marriage. I'm not sure if I understand."

"Courting protects guys and gals from doing stupid things. If we end this relationship without ever kissing, then I can tell my future wife someday that she is the first girl I ever kissed. Satan wants you and I to mix it up every time we see each other. God's sacred gift of sex is strictly for the marriage bed between a man and a woman."

"But a kiss isn't sex."

"Yes, but it sure can lead to it! Answer, if you wish, have you ever kissed a guy on a date?"

She hesitated as she looked away from me. "Ah, yes."

"Do you look back on that kiss with so much love in your heart that you're super glad you kissed that guy? Or do you look back and think the kiss has no value anymore?"

"I never thought about it till now, but it really means nothing."

"So, Judy, I'm thinking a couple more times of courting and then I will tell you if I want to continue or end the courting part of it. Who knows, maybe I want to continue and you don't."

"This seems strange to me, Jude. I want to think on this some more."

We packed up our lunch items and mounted Pete and Joe to head around the block. When we got to the edge of the woods, three black vultures slowly circled up ahead.

"Judy, do you see the vultures?"

"Yep, they're kind of neat in a way, but kind of ugly too."

"I wonder what they're hanging around for?" I said as we rode along the edge of the gravel road.

It wasn't long before our noses informed us of what we were riding past: a big bloated doe laying alongside the road: flies, maggots, vultures and stink all in one package. Pete and Joe even reacted to it the closer we got. I kissed to Joe to trot so we could get to the other side sooner.

"Wow! That's enough to make a grown man cry!" Judy laughed.

"What kind of saying is that?" I asked.

"My dad always says it when things get bad."

"That's a pretty good one," I added.

Judy spoke more of her relationship with her parents and how she admired my parents and Becky. She also talked of her old self before Christ and how bad she felt for all the things she had done. I simply reminded her not to look into the past but to look at God's plans from today forward.

"Speaking of the future," I asked, "how many kids do you want to have?"

"What?" she hollered. "First you won't even kiss me and now you're talking about how many kids to have?"

"I didn't say I would be the dad."

"Four."

"Girls or boys?"

"Both."

"City or country living?"

"Small farm."

I was thinking on the next question when she asked, "Minivan or SUV?"

"Do I have to be practical, Judy?"

"Yep."

"Minivan."

"What color?"

"Black like the geldings, of course."

"Nope, maroon or nothing."

We were just about to our driveway when I heard the loud exhaust pipes heading our way. Pete and Joe tensed up as they shot their ears backwards to try to judge what was coming. Greg Shants was heading our way very fast.

"Spin Pete around and face the noise!" I yelled to Judy as I did the same with Joe.

The geldings had a look of terror in their eyes as the truck got closer. "Easy boys, easy!" I hollered, trying to calm them. Greg saw us and hugged the edge of the road as he roared past us, shooting gravel our way. Pete and Joe spun around in a couple tight circles as Judy and I hung on.

"Whoa boys, whoa. Now settle down! You remember that truck from before. It's not going to hurt you."

"Wow that was pretty hairy, Jude. I didn't know what was going to happen." Judy sighed.

"Hey, you did very well to stay on, maybe you should join the PBR."

"What's that?"

"The big rodeo you see on TV."

Pete and Joe pranced the rest of the way home. I helped Judy down off Pete and had to laugh. She was stiff from riding so long and could hardly walk. As she stretched out I started untacking the geldings. Judy curried Pete and led him to the pasture while I did the same with Joe. We stood there and watched them roll on the bare ground.

"Judy, thank you for coming with today. You did very well in how you handled Pete. I enjoyed it and I hope you did. By the way, I have a cousin getting married in three weeks and I was wondering if you would go with me. There's a wedding dance afterward. I'll call you and let you know the details."

"Okay, I will see. I really did enjoy riding Pete. He was so good. I'd better go."

"Judy, you might want to practice your whistle for Pete and Joe. Who knows, someday you might need it. Maybe you just like shoveling poop!"

With that she took off after me a few steps and realized she was still stiff. She stood and smiled as I ran away. I have to say I was feeling very good about courting Judy.

I lay in bed that night going over the horse ride with Judy. I wondered if the geldings would ever come to someone else's whistle. I gradually dozed off with good thoughts dancing in my head. Unfortunately my dreams were not good, that same nightmare was back. I think I was in some type of hospital bed. Greg Shants was in shackles and an orange prison suit, yet he seemed to have even more power than before. Mom was losing it. I would talk with her but she just looked right through me as if I wasn't even there. For some reason Mr. Olson was loading the geldings in his horse trailer, and they didn't want to go. I was yelling at Pete and Joe to settle down. It was so intense, I actually woke myself calling, "Pete, Joe!" I was all sweaty from the dream and couldn't get back to sleep the rest of the night. What was going on?

In three weeks, it was time to pick up Judy for my cousin's wedding. I washed and vacuumed out the van and headed her way.

Mrs. Clemons answered the door. "Oh, it's you!" She then yelled upstairs. "Judy your date is here."

"Thank you, Mrs. Clemons."

She stood and stared, as if angry at me. "Judy says I need to invite you for Sunday dinner. Does tomorrow work for you?"

"Church ends at noon, so I guess I could come over right after that. Thank you."

Judy came bouncing down the steps with that gleam in her eyes. We said our goodbyes to her mom and headed to the wedding.

"I looked up courting on the net and agree with what you said, Jude. So this is number three. Is Sunday dinner number four?"

"I think Sunday counts for a half of one, so I vote we go to a movie together as the other half. What do you think?"

"Yep."

The wedding was very nice. It was the first Christian wedding Judy had been to. She asked a few questions about it afterward. The dance reception was great. The DJ had old- fashioned Appalachian square dancing mixed in with some sixties era slow and fast dances. The square dancing was a blast! The floor was packed each time the DJ called for squares. Judy seemed to have a great time also. I watched her smile and mingle with my relatives. I do believe I was building feelings toward Judy with each date.

On the way home I suggested, "Since I chose this event, how about you pick a movie and a night and let me know what time to pick you up?"

"Sounds fair to me." She continued, "Jude, what are you doing for college or work this fall?"

"Right now I'm scheduled to head west to take a one-year Bible course. After that I'll come back home and go to a natural hoof trimming school. What are your plans?"

"What is a natural hoof trimming school?"

"Natural hoof trimming school is where you learn to trim a horse's foot the way God intended with no iron shoes and nails that don't allow the horse's foot to flex."

"I'm hoping to get into Crown College for their nursing program. It's a four-year program, and I feel a nurse is always going to be able to find work."

"Good for you, Judy! A nurse is a great goal and I'm sure you'll make a good one someday." We pulled into her driveway. "Did you want to go to church with me in the morning and then back here for lunch?"

"Oh, I better not. That might qualify for date number four, and besides, I'll need to help Mom with dinner."

"Okay, see ya tomorrow after church. Is there anything I need to bring?"

"Just a smile."

"God bless."

As I drove home I ran through what tomorrow might bring in my mind. "God, I ask you for guidance with Judy and I. The more I see her the more I want to see her. I pray for pure motives, Lord, and that this relationship will glorify you." I drove on reminiscing about Judy at the wedding reception and how good it felt to introduce her to relatives.

After church the next day I pulled into Judy's driveway for Sunday dinner. Mr. Clemons was sitting on the front porch. "Good morning, Judd. Have a seat here with me. Lunch isn't quite ready. How was church this morning, Judd?"

"Oh, it was fine, sir."

"Ya see, Judd, not everyone needs church and besides, most of the people that go to church are a bunch of hypocrites."

I surprised Mr. Clemons with my next statement. "Yes, sir, in fact, all people that go to my church are hypocrites and sinners."

He sat there stymied, and cleared his throat. "Yes, Judd, us Clemons don't need church. We are basically good people and try to do our best, so sin is not really a problem here."

"With all due respect, Mr. Clemons, the Bible states that all have sinned and fallen short of the glory of God. I'm a sinner and am thankful for what Jesus did on the cross for me."

"Yeah, yeah, you can keep your Jesus in your pocket while you're here. Is that something we can agree on?"

"I've met you twice now, Mr. Clemons, and I can respect that you have opinions but I don't have to agree with them. Please remember, I'm not the one that has brought Jesus into the conversations."

After that we sat in silence for the longest time as Mr. Clemons stared into the yard, expressionless. I rehashed the conversation in my mind and was glad I didn't allow Mr. Clemons to push me to deny Jesus Christ's existence.

I decided to break the silence. "Mr. Clemons, I really didn't get a chance to ask your permission to spend time with Judy, so I'm asking now. Can I spend time with your daughter?"

He sat there stammering for an answer with a puzzled look on his face. Just then Judy burst onto the scene announcing that dinner was served. "Dad, Jude, dinner is ready, get in here right away before the dinner rolls cool down."

I had to laugh to myself as we walked in. Mr. Clemons was mumbling my name. "Jude? Judd? What the..."

As we sat down, Judy announced it was prayer time. I had a hard time not looking Mr. Clemons' way to see his response. From the corner of my eye I saw him slowly fold his hands. "Father God, we thank you for this beautiful Sunday. We ask that you bless our company today, and we thank you for this wonderful meal you have provided for us, Lord Jesus. Amen."

Mrs. Clemons had made a Sunday dinner that I'll not soon forget. Some type of burnt hot dish, lumpy mashed potatoes, and cream-style corn that tasted like wallpaper paste. I struggled through that meal and drank lots of milk until they ran out, then gulped water like a camel. It's amazing how little food a guy can get by on when you have to.

Mr. Clemons was mostly silent during the meal. Mrs. Clemons looked my way, "What good are those big horses you have. They just seem like a lot of work." She spoke with her mouth full of food.

"Not sure if I can explain it Mrs. Clemons, but I've always wanted Percherons ever since I was in grade school."

Every once in a while I would make eye contact with Judy and she'd smile. Mrs. Clemons spoke for Mr. Clemons quite a bit that day. The air was heavy with the smell of burnt hot dish.

As Judy and her mom were getting dessert, Mr. Clemons blurted out as he looked my way, "Thank you for helping Judy out last winter when she got stuck in the snow bank. I was tied up that day and couldn't get there."

"You're more than welcome, Mr. Clemons."

He was still looking my way when he said, "Yes, Judd, I mean Jude, you can date Judy, as long as you promise to take care of her."

"I promise, sir. Thank you."

Judy and her mom were just bringing the green jello with apple slices mixed in as I said 'I promise.' Not sure about you but green jello is bad enough on its own, than to add hard apples to it, Yuck! Of course Mrs. Clemons scoops up a huge bowl for me. I tell you it took will power to down that mountain.

"Mrs. Clemons, I thank you for having me over," I said as I bit my lip to keep a straight face.

"Oh, yes Judy told me I should invite you." As she dug in her teeth with her finger. "You sure didn't eat much, that hot dish is a family tradition. Would you like to take some home?"

I glanced at Judy, then back to Mrs. Clemons. "No ma'am, that's okay you can save it for yourselves. It's something I'll never forget."

Judy and I told her mom that she could take a break and we would clean up the kitchen. I could tell Judy was curious as to her Dad's statement to me about promising to take care of her.

After dishes I pushed Judy on the board swing they had out on the cottonwood tree. To the west a big thunderstorm was brewing as Judy glided back and forth in the swing. It seemed like Judy's pace was in time with the thunder and lightning. "Dad always talks of thunderstorms as if God is telling us something." I looked west at the beautiful show God was providing.

Judy tried to get me to tell her what I promised her dad, but I figured that was really between him and me. It was soon time to leave for chores. As I said goodbye, I reminded Judy to call me for the movie night.

I opened the mail two days later and there was a fancy looking envelope addressed to me that smelled of perfume. I knew right away it was from Judy. I stood out by the mailbox as I opened it. "Dear Jude, you will be picked up next Friday night at 5:30 sharp by a beautiful Princess for a night of dining and a lovely movie. Please wear your Wrangler jeans and your light pink shirt and bring an appetite and the proper attitude for enjoying a CHICK FLICK with Judy Clemons. P.S. – Remember what the Bible says about complaining. Signed, Judy."

I was sitting on the front porch that Friday at twenty after five waiting for Judy. At exactly 5:30 I heard the tires coming across the gravel driveway. Judy stepped out and came to the front porch without seeing me. She rang the door bell as I sat there silently.

"Can I help you?"

I startled her for a second. "Why yes, I'm here to pick up Mr. Jude Bonner for a very important date. Have you seen him?"

"That mainly depends on this movie you have picked out. Ya know a guy has to be careful about watching too many chick flicks. They say it can affect his status as a cowboy!"

"You tell Mr. Bonner that one or two chick flicks will only enhance his cowboy status. Now give me your arm and walk me to the car."

Judy took us to a small cafe in Spicer where we had big juicy burgers, onion rings, barbeque wings and chocolate milk shakes. After supper we had extra time so we walked along Green Lake until it was time to head to the Spicer Theaters. Judy wasn't kidding about a "chick flick." She loved it, but even though I didn't tell her, I thought it was a little strange. It just reaffirms how God made man and woman differently. Thank you Lord!

Chapter 3
"The Stearns County Fair"

Our phone rang. Mom answered. "Jude, it's for you."

"Hello." It was Mr. Olson.

"Jude, I've been thinking and wondering if you have ever thought about taking them geldings to the Stearns County Fair? They have a strong Draft horse show on Saturday night and they even have a halter class. I would love to see how Pete and Joe do in the halter class."

"That does sound pretty neat, Mr. Olson. I never thought about that. Do you know what the entry fee might be?"

"If you are willing to take them up there, I'll gladly pay any entry fees for you. Not sure if you know Clyde Devon from Melrose, but he has some real nice Percheron geldings that he shows every year. Pete and Joe would have their work cut out for them. Clyde has put together four geldings that have plenty of space between the ground and their bellies and are heads up flashy."

"Wow! That could be interesting, Mr. Olson. Do you think Pete and Joe could win?"

"That's hard to say. It's been years since I was in that racket. Stan Blanchard is sometimes the judge and he's raised Percherons for years and sold some awful good ones in that time. You think it over and let me know if I need to help. Goodbye."

Becky was reading in the living room when I got off the phone, Fuzz sleeping by her feet. "Becky, are you willing to braid the geldings for the Stearns County Fair the first part of August?" "What! Are you kidding? That would be awesome! Sure, let's do it!"

"Thanks, I think we need to go over to Mr. Olson's and ask him more questions tomorrow. You know he used to help a couple friends show drafts at the State fair?"

The phone started ringing again. "I'll get it, it must be Mr. Olson again." I answered with a statement right away. "Yes we're going!" There was silence at the other end.

"Jude?"

"I'm sorry Judy! I thought it was Mr. Olson."

"That's okay, do I need to call back later?"

"No, you're fine. How you doing?"

She was silent for awhile. "Oh, I just wanted to hear your voice, Jude."

"What's the matter?"

"I don't know. It's just that..." She stopped again. "Mom and Dad have been drinking again. They're downstairs and I'm in my bedroom. I just feel like an idiot when they do this, and then I call you! I'm sorry, Jude."

"That's okay, Judy. Do you need me to come over or anything?"

"No, no, it's okay. I've been in this place many times before, but it helps to hear your voice, thank you."

"Are you sure?"

"Yes, I'm fine."

"I want you to know I had a great time at your movie and dinner the other night. I'm a little worried though."

"How come?"

"Do you realize how many action movies it will take to get my cowboy status back?"

She chuckled a little. "You know you liked that movie just as much as I did, you're just not man enough to admit it."

"Ouch! I have to admit, it was maybe a little better than I expected."

"Now, what do you and Mr. Olson have going on?"

"How did you know we had something in the works? I just hung up the phone with him."

"Oh women's intuition, and I'm starting to know you better, so it has to be something with horses, am I correct?"

I laughed as I sat there. "Guilty as charged! Mr. Olson is suggesting we take the geldings to the Stearns County Fair in August. Who knows, I just might take you to the fair for our next date?"

"I'd love to go, Jude! I haven't been to a county fair since I was a little kid. Maybe I could help with Pete and Joe?"

"Becky and I are going over to his place tomorrow to ask more questions. I can let you know more later."

"Yep."

Judy and I talked for another forty five minutes before we hung up. I had a hard time believing that I spent that much time on the phone with a girl. What was going on?

"I think I see wedding bells in the future!" Becky laughed as I hung up the phone.

"What are you talking about, wedding bells? It will be years before you see Jude Bonner saying 'I do.' "

"Nope, you're wrong. It will happen sooner rather than later. I'll have Pete and Joe braided up extra fancy for the big day."

"Who says you'll even be invited to such a prestigious event? By the time I get married, Pete and Joe will be too old to pull anything."

I did my devotions and went to bed. The buzz of mosquitoes against the screen was constant as I lay there thinking of the fair. All of a sudden I jumped to the side as a loud howling shot into my ears. Fuzz stood by the window and softly growled. "Fuzz, I think they're a little more than you can handle!" Coyotes were howling to each other in what seemed just yards away from my window. That screeching howl was a little creepy as they went up and down the music scale. I always wonder how many are howling at one time. It's surprising how short they howl. A minute later all you could hear was the skeeters at the screen again.

Becky and I went to Mr. Olson's place after chores the next morning to talk Stearns County Fair. He seemed all excited as he handed me a list he had written up.

"Take a look at that and see what you think. It's what I could think of to get ready for the big show." He continued, "I would practice setting Pete and Joe in a show stance a couple times a week. We'll set Ladd up for you, so you know what to look for."

We walked out to the pasture with a halter and lead rope and got a hold of Ladd. "Now Jude, you have to realize that Ladd is a finely tuned hitch gelding that could be the lead horse in most hitches. So I don't want you to get too discouraged!" He laughed as Ladd plodded along behind him.

Becky and I both took turns setting Ladd up for a proper stance for the halter class. Ladd was so lazy, it was hard to do. Mr. Olson tried to get him excited by snapping a whip behind him, but Ladd had his own pace. We would trot him and turn him, then set his feet so he would look his best. I had to laugh as Becky tried to get him to hold his head up. He rubbed the side of his face against Becky and knocked her sideways. I looked over at Mr. Olson as he smiled at the whole event.

Becky and I were soon leading Pete and Joe out and competing against each other in our yard. I took Joe, and Becky led Pete. They were definitely way more lively than Ladd, especially Joe. Becky even talked Mom into being a judge one time. I was sure to win because Joe was more animated at the trot. Mom studied each of us and awarded Becky with the win: a gift certificate to the Blue Banana.

"Hey, that ain't fair!" I hollered as Becky was all smiles.

"I don't know what the judge will do Jude, but that is the way I see it happening." Mom said.

"Joe, you aren't going to let them win at the fair, are you big guy?" I gave him a big hug. "Becky, they hand out cash to the winners at the fair. That's much better than a gift certificate!"

The closer we got to the fair, the more nervous I was. I trimmed their feet extra nice and we tried to keep them out of the sun so they wouldn't fade so bad. We were soon loading them into the trailer for the trip north to Sauk Centre. With all the stuff we had to take, you'd think we were moving in! I had sleeping stuff along so I could be close to the geldings, since this was their first trip to a fair. Mr. Olson and Becky would drive back and forth.

The fair grounds were swarming with people and animals. The weather wasn't ideal; it was about 95 degrees and very humid. We eased our way through the gate, and Pete and Joe started to whinny as we headed toward the draft horse barn.

"Why certainly, we'll see what these boys are made of. You lead one and I'll lead the other. Pay close attention, you never know how they will react," cautioned Mr. Olson.

Pete and Joe stomped their feet hard on the trailer floor as we stepped out of the pickup. "Easy boys, easy."

As I opened the back gate, Joe danced side to side and watched every move I made. "Joe settle down, easy now." I spoke softly trying to calm him. I slowly placed my hand on his big rump and tried to push him to one side. He was not in the mood to cooperate! He stood his ground as he cocked his head, looking at me from the corner of his eye.

"JOE, GET YOUR BUTT OVER!" I yelled.

He finally eased over to the right and allowed me room to slide up to his tie rope. I rubbed his neck as I untied him. "Okay Joe, back." Joe starting snorting as he backed up very slowly.

"Jude, keep backing him for awhile after he is out of the trailer." Mr. Olson said as he stood beside the trailer.

"Step down Joe, easy boy, step back." Joe fought me a little as we backed; he wanted to turn around in the trailer. "Joe, you're backing out of this trailer if it takes me all day."

With his back feet right at the edge of the step, he put the brakes on. He had had enough! I immediately put back pressure on the lead rope. I bet we stood there for two minutes before he figured that rope halter wasn't feeling good across the bridge of his nose. He slowly lowered his right back foot on the ground and then his left. Guess what, he put the brakes on again! I put back pressure on and he soon tried turning. I pulled his head back straight and kept the pressure on the rope halter. He gradually eased back and was out of the trailer. He wanted to spin right away, but I kept him going backward. I pushed him back for nearly 50 yards.

'Whoa!" Joe stopped and I rubbed his neck with the butt end of the whip. I led him forward back toward the trailer as he snorted and pranced. There was quite a crowd gathered for this show. I stood beside the trailer as Becky backed Pete out. Of course, Pete came out like a champ and the crowd applauded. Pete stood there like this was old news.

"Thanks Becky. Did you really have to make me look that bad?"

"No problem, wait till halter class!"

"Gee, thanks!"

We led Pete and Joe into the draft horse barn and found our stalls. Joe was nervous, but with Pete right beside him he was doing okay. We tied them up and gave them some hay to keep them occupied while we carried the rest of the stuff in. Mr. Olson put the truck away while Becky and I registered them for halter class. As we came back to the barn, a short stocky muscular man was standing right behind Pete and Joe.

"Hello, I'm Clyde Devon."

"I'm Jude and this is my sister Becky."

"Don't tell me I have to compete with these two boys in halter class. Why, I might as well pack up the boys and go home!" He laughed. "How old are they?"

"Pete and Joe are four year olds."

"Pete and Joe you say? Pretty nice, yes sir, pretty nice. Well, if you need anything, let me know. I'm just across the aisle."

I was walking tall, as they say, until I looked across the aisle at Clyde's geldings. Mr. Olson was right, they had a lot of leg under them. Clyde had his stalls all decorated with bright ribbons and his ranch name, very classy! We certainly had our work cut out for us.

I looked down the aisle and there came Judy heading our way. She was all smiles as she approached us. "Judy, what are you doing here?" I asked.

"I came to help and besides, after riding Pete, he's my buddy!"

I smiled as I noticed the gleam in her eyes. "How about you and Becky sit on them and work on their manes?"

"I get to do Pete." Judy called out.

"Joe, I guess you're stuck with me." Becky laughed.

"I'll boost each of you up there. Are you ready?" I clasped my hands together and sent Becky up first and then Judy. Wow, I was kind of pleased with the ease of lifting them. I could tell my push-ups and pull-ups were working. Becky and Judy drew a lot of attention from the fair goers as they sat on the geldings. Soon they were each laying on their stomachs with their heads over Pete and Joe's rumps, talking with people as they passed. It seemed like everyone took a picture with their cell phones.

I was over talking with Clyde when Greg Shants came strolling in. He stood in the center of the aisle and pretended he didn't see me. He reached into his pocket and put a cigarette in his mouth as he was surrounded by "NO SMOKING" signs. As he reached for a lighter I had had enough. I walked up behind him and grabbed the cigarette out of his mouth, crushing it in my hands. Greg spun around to confront me as we were only inches away from each other in a stare down. I had each fist clenched and was hoping he would take it to the next level. He stunk like I never smelled before and had a faraway look in his eyes.

Clyde walked over. "Boys, this is not the time or place." He looked directly at Greg. "See that door down there, Sonny? The sooner you use it the better, now get going."

Greg slowly walked away with a smirk on his face and reached for a second cigarette. "Don't you even think about it!" Clyde yelled. "Keep moving."

Clyde and I stood in the center of the aisle until Greg was out of sight. "I have to assume that isn't your first rodeo with that clown."

"Nope, we went to high school together and have had several rodeos. In fact, I hate to say it, he won the last one."

"I hope you didn't mind me stepping in when I did?"

"No, that was fine. Who knows how long we would have stood there."

I looked over to Judy and Becky and they each gave me a thumbs-up. I soon had several piles to clean up behind Pete and Joe while Becky and Judy sat in lawn chairs answering all the questions from the people. It was funny to listen to people as they walk past. They thought Pete and Joe and the other drafts were huge! I guess we got used to how big they are and thought nothing of it.

Every once in awhile I would bring Pete out to the aisle and let a couple little kids sit on his back. To watch their little eyes get as big as saucers and huge smiles was special. The best one was a little girl with Down's Syndrome. Her parents were a little reluctant to put her up there, but I could tell she wasn't leaving until that happened. I swooped her up onto Pete, stood back, and watched. The expression on her face was priceless. She sat there very still at first, but soon she was hugging Pete as she softly stroked his neck with her little hands. Pete knew she was special and stood dead still as she sat there. She started to talk to him and his ears shot back her direction. He even gave her a soft nicker back. He would shake his head up and down as she spoke to him in a language only the two of them understood. I looked back at her parents and they both had tears streaming down their faces. Next thing I knew, I was wiping my eyes. As I lifted her down, I couldn't help but give her a hug as I fought back tears. As she walked back to her parents, she stopped and hugged Pete's left hind leg. He turned his head and gave another soft nicker, his way of saying goodbye. Becky took a few pictures of the whole episode.

"You've got a very special girl there." I paused to wipe more tears. "Pete doesn't even talk to me that way, and I'm his owner."

"We thank you so much for your kindness. You don't know how much this means to her."

"Don't thank me, Pete did all the work."

"Come on Kelly, we have to get to the other barns."

I looked back at her and she gave Pete a big kiss on his hock and walked back to her parents. I knelt down beside her. "Kelly, thank you for being so kind to Pete. You ask your parents to bring you back tomorrow and you can ride him with a saddle."

She looked at me with her big brown eyes and then at her parents as she teared up. She reached her arms out for a hug from me, and I was losing it. She hugged me and ran back, giving Pete one more leg hug before running to her dad's arms.

"See ya tomorrow."

"Why certainly, if that don't beat all!" Mr. Olson stood there shaking his head as they left. "It's not very often a guy goes to the county fair and cries like a baby! That was special Jude. Well I think you're set here, so Becky and I are heading south. We'll be back after chores in the morning. Call me if you need anything. Night."

Judy and I sat there behind the geldings and talked till 11:30. I found it so easy to talk with her. Her summer job in Belgrade was at the convenience store. She had plenty of stories to tell of all the different customers who came in. She had to deal with shop lifters, gas spills, and people leaving without paying for their gas. She talked more of her parents and her upbringing. Come to find out, Judy wasn't an only child; her parents had twin girls who only lived about a week. Judy was only three at the time so she didn't remember it. She asked me to go to the grave site with her someday. We talked about Greg Shants and his little display of stupidity.

"Judy, do you realize what time it is?"

"Yes I do, I suppose I'd better get going. I'm staying at my Aunt Sarah's place, here in Sauk, so I don't have to drive all the way home. Jude, thank you for this evening, I'll be back tomorrow sometime to check in on Pete and Joe."

"What do you mean, Pete and Joe. What about me!"

"Hey, buddy, we're not past our four dates yet, so you need to fend for yourself!"

I walked Judy to her car and said good night. I walked back to check the geldings one last time and headed to my tent. I was tired. I lay there absorbing all the sounds of the fair: the demo derby just finishing up, the carnival music, kids screaming on the rides, cows bellering, and the horses shuffling in their stalls. I thanked the Lord and slid off to sleep.

Boy did I dream all sorts of crazy things that night. I was in a runaway hot air balloon. I was being chased by Frankenstein as Dad stood and watched, and I was the main bad guy in a nationwide man hunt. I finally started dreaming about Pete and Joe. You'd think that would be good, but no, this was different. I'm not sure why, but they were in some sort of trouble. I heard them whinny time and time again, but I couldn't find them anywhere. I couldn't tell what, but it seemed they were fighting something? Their screams for help got louder as I finally shook myself awake all sweaty. I had to tell myself I was only dreaming, but their calls for help were still there. It took a couple seconds to realize where I was and that Pete and Joe were in trouble.

I slipped on my boots and flew out of that tent, heading toward the draft horse barn as fast as I could run. I rounded the corner and there stood Greg Shants with a whip in his hand, wailing on their rumps and laughing. Pete and Joe were kicking out and had a look of terror in their eyes. I totally lost it! No one was going to do this to my horses.

I ran full blast and tackled Greg down onto the ground. I straddled him and started throwing punches into his face. He tried to block them and get out from under me, but it wasn't working. I was overwhelmed with strength and quickness. Most of my punches were meeting his face.

All of a sudden, I was pulled off by someone. It was Bill Masters! He held my arms behind me as Greg slowly stood up. "Well Bible boy, haven't we been in this position before? I'm going to take you apart piece by piece." With that said, Bill spun me around and punched me towards Greg. Greg punched me back to Bill. I was a human tether ball!

I went back and forth a couple times until I caught a glimpse of Clyde Devon coming to the rescue. He took hold of Bill with a head lock and slammed him into a post. Bill let out a huge moan and slumped to the ground. Greg and I were so surprised we actually stopped fighting and watched this all take place. Clyde knelt down and held him by the collar, slapped him on the cheek and said, "Now you sit there quietly or I'll finish this fight." Clyde looked back at me. "What are you waiting for?" Greg and I squared up with fists clenched. I heard Pete and Joe in the background, like they were cheering for me. I will never forget the look on his face, like he wasn't even in his body! I faked a left and came with a right roundhouse that caught him square on his chin. His long greasy hair flew back from the force. I followed it with some hard punches to his stomach. I stood back thinking he was done after those hits, but next thing I knew he was right back at me like my punches had no power. He threw his shoulder into my gut and drove me back into an empty stall. His strength seemed supernatural. I had heard of guys on drugs having unbelievable power, and that is what I was up against.

Greg had me pinned against the wall as I rained down on his back with my clenched fists. I was swinging super hard and it didn't faze him. He was squeezing the breath out of me and I was getting nowhere fast. I reached down and grabbed some fresh horse crap and started shoving it into his mouth as he gasped for air. Greg dropped his grip on me and started to spit and sputter. He was still bent over so I grabbed his head and brought my knee up into his face several times. I threw him out into the aisle, again thinking he couldn't take anymore. He got right back up like I never even hit him!

"When I'm done with you, then it will be Judy's turn you piece of s..."

"By the power of Jesus' name I'll defeat you Satan!" I screamed at the top of my lungs!

All of a sudden I had the strength of Samson. I looked at the bulging veins in my arms and, with God on my side, I started throwing punches. One after the other, and I never missed his face once. He staggered back with each punch but still wasn't going down. My punches were stopping him from swinging back but he was still acting like this wasn't hurting him. The onslaught continued as blood spewed from his face with each blow.

He was gradually showing signs of getting weaker. I wasn't going to stop till he was laying on the ground. I took a few steps back and came with a right that sent him to his knees. I took more steps back and lined him up for a size 12 to the face. I never felt so much rage in my life! I planted the heel of my boot right square on his nose. I stood back to get ready and saw him wavering as his nose looked like hamburger. I got ready to plant another but I could tell it was over. I stood and watched as Greg slumped over in the aisle.

Pete and Joe were still nervous from what Greg had done to them. I walked behind them and started talking to them as they were dancing back and forth. "Easy boys, easy, it's okay now, easy."

Clyde came over and stood by me. "I think they're more scared then hurt, Jude."

Clyde and I ran our hands over their rumps to feel for any cuts or abrasions. "Jude, I think we should take them for a walk right after the cops get here. When you were fighting some lady came by and called 911."

Sure enough, the bright blue beacons of a patrol car were heading our way. The cops met us in the aisle by Greg. They put Greg in cuffs right away and then asked who had done this. I raised my hand, and next thing I knew I was in cuffs, too.

"Officer, may I sit down while you go over this?" I asked.

"Sure, have a seat on the bale over there. You will probably have to go back to the station while we get both stories."

"Officer, I'm Clyde Devon and I'm willing to vouch for this young man. If that helps at all."

"We'll see, now what is your name?" He had a clip board and was writing.

"Jude Bonner."

He asked my age, address, my parents' names, if I had been drinking, and what started the fight.

"Greg and I have been going at it since high school, so when I came in and saw him whipping Pete and Joe," I pointed at the geldings, "why, why I just plain lost it! I dove into him and started throwing punches."

The cop looked at Clyde and Clyde nodded his head in agreement.

"Do you know Greg's last name?"

"Yes, sir, Shants. It's Greg Shants."

The cop got a puzzled look on his face. "Did I hear you correctly, 'Greg Shants'?"

"Yes sir."

He asked his partner to get the bulletin off the dash of the squad car. "I think we may have hit the jackpot!"

His partner gave him the bulletin and they both scanned it very closely. "Mr. Bonner, I want to congratulate you on your fine police work tonight!"

I looked at Clyde first and then the police officer with a puzzled look. Clyde looked puzzled too. "What do you mean 'police work'?"

He waved the bulletin. "Greg Shants is a wanted fugitive and has eluded law enforcement for the last two weeks. The bulletin states that he could be armed and dangerous, and is wanted for burglary, assault with a deadly weapon, and drug charges."

Clyde piped in. "If there is any reward just send it to my address, please."

The officers loaded Greg in the back of the squad car and left. Luckily, they took my cuffs off before they left. I sat there inspecting my knuckles as Clyde went to get some ice.

"Jude, for a minute I thought I was going to have to step in for you and tag team that Greg guy. I've never seen anyone take punches like that and come back for more!"

"I thank you for taking Bill out of the fight. I don't think I could have beat both of them."

"That's okay, it's been awhile since I've had that much fun. Isn't that what you come to the fair for, is fun." He laughed.

"Clyde, I thank you again, but, sorry to say, this afternoon in halter class Pete and Joe will be taking all the rewards home. You might even consider just keeping your horses in their stalls to save you any embarrassment."

"Now them's fighting words young man, and I think you're all fought out!" Clyde joked as he shadow boxed a little. "We'll let the judge decide who takes home the hardware. I do look forward to the competition and wish you the best. Ice those hands some more and keep flexing them so they don't get too stiff. Maybe I need to be your trainer for the MMA?"

"Yeah, right!" I laughed.

I sat there a little longer with the ice on my knuckles and thought about Greg and what was in store for him. I thanked God and got up to clean horse stalls. Clyde and I ate breakfast at the 4-H booth, and he even gave me some pointers for halter class.

When I got back to the barn, Becky and Mr. Olson were brushing the geldings.

"I'll bet you slept like a rock last night and didn't have anything exciting happen. Why certainly."

"Yes sir, it was very boring, slept right through the night

without any interruptions."

"Okay kids, you need to walk these guys around a little so they don't get bound up in the gut."

"Mr. Olson, do you want to lead one?"

"No, I have something to do right now, you and Becky take them."

Becky backed Pete out and I followed with Joe. "Jude, thanks for letting me work with these guys as much as you do. I really appreciate it."

"Becky, these guys wouldn't be the horses they are if it weren't for you, and I thank you for that."

Becky and I trotted them and practiced like we were in halter class. We took them half way around the grounds and brought them back to their stalls. Mr. Olson and Judy had a surprise waiting for us when we got back. Pete and Joe's stall was all decorated with fancy colored head liner and their names were on wooden boards. Judy was all smiles as we approached.

"Judy, this is beautiful! When did you think of it?" I asked.

"After seeing Clyde's set up, I figured it was time to keep up with the Devons."

Becky asked, "Who made the wooden things with their names on them?"

"My dad did. Jude, he wanted to do this for you!"

"This is totally awesome! Pete and Joe, what do you think of what Judy did to your stall?"

Joe snorted softly as the ribbons tussled with the breeze. We took some pictures with all of us in front of our newly remodeled horse stalls.

"Judy and Becky, are you ready to scrub the geldings spotless?"

Judy was all smiles. "You mean I can help?"

"You and Becky lead them out to the wash rack and I'll bring the buckets and soap."

I had to stand and watch as they led the geldings out. They were two mighty proud ladies! Mr. Olson and I gathered up the bath supplies and headed to the wash rack. Becky and Judy washed Pete while I did Joe. I'm just not sure how it happened, but each time I hosed the geldings off, a little extra spray went Judy and Becky's way. It wasn't long and I was hit by a soapy sponge in the face. Mr. Olson burst out laughing. It was soon a full fledged water war. The only problem I had was that it was two against one! It actually felt pretty good. I was still kind of grimy from the fight with Greg, and it was hot outside. I wasn't totally sure if the geldings got clean, but we had a good time getting wet!

Becky and Judy led them back to their stalls as I picked up the cleaning supplies. We let them dry somewhat, and Mr. Olson and Becky started to braid their tails as Judy and I untangled their manes. I'll never forget what Mr. Olson did as he was braiding a tail, when someone asked a common question as they passed by.

"How old are they?"

Without looking back at them, Mr. Olson raised the tail and studied Pete's exhaust hole for awhile and said, '8 years,' and kept right on braiding without looking back. That's all it took for Becky. She lost it right there; she was going crazy trying not to laugh. I looked at Mr. Olson and he had a gleam in his eye. "Why certainly."

I kept an eye on what Clyde was doing and noticed he wasn't braiding his geldings. This would give me an edge. Yes, I already had the blue ribbon in my hands before the halter class even started. We noticed the judge pass through the barn on his way to the arena. Becky led Pete and I had Joe. There were only six geldings in our class, Clyde had four and then Pete and Joe. I ran the end results through my mind. Joe would be number one, with Pete or one of Clyde's coming in second. The rest really didn't matter.

The judge had us stand and set our horses, and then we each had to lead them at a trot towards him and away from him. I'm not sure why, but the judge felt all their front feet for something. He stood back and scanned the whole group. I knew Joe and I had it in the bag. He called out one of Clyde's geldings first. What? "Of course, he is starting with the last place first," I thought to myself as I glanced at Becky. Becky and Pete were called and then finally Joe and I. My smile was wider than the Mississippi as I proudly brought Joe into the line-up again. The assistant brought the ribbons to the judge. He took one last look and headed the wrong way! I about broke my neck as I turned to watch the judge hand Clyde my blue ribbon. To add insult to injury, there were only three ribbons. Pete and Joe came in dead last, braided manes and all. The judge stood talking with Clyde as if we didn't even exist! Becky and I stood there bewildered. I was slowly grasping what took place and really wasn't liking the truth. I looked over to Mr. Olson as he turned and walked toward the barn. I went into rationalization mode and decided the judge had something against us, or maybe he was Clyde's neighbor or uncle or brother.

I dragged my butt toward the barn as Joe followed, and Mr. Olson met me at the door.

"Sorry Jude, I know you're disappointed."

I didn't even answer him back. I was mad.

"Let me take Joe for you so you can go talk with the judge."

"Why would I go talk with him? He just ruined my day! He must be half blind or something."

Mr. Olson got pretty stern. "Instead of complaining about the judge, get back there and ask why. You actually might learn something, maybe the truth."

I looked at Becky and Judy standing there listening and felt very foolish. I thought about it for a little as I really didn't want to talk with someone that I thought was wrong.

Judy grabbed my arm. "Come on, I'll go with you."

The judge was walking our way as we turned around. "Sir, I have some questions on that last halter class," I said with a hint of anger. I was going to teach this guy a thing or two!

"Hi, I'm Fred Billings." He extended his arm and we shook hands. "I bet you're wondering why I placed you where I did?"

"Yes, this is my first halter class and I just don't understand!"

He looked me in the eye and then at Judy. "May I ask your names?"

"Oh sorry, Jude Bonner and this is Judy Clemons."

"Okay Jude, do you understand what a halter class is trying to accomplish?"

I stammered a bit. "Well, not real sure, I guess."

"First of all, your geldings looked very nice with the braids and ribbons. A halter class is confirmation only, braids and ribbons really don't add to confirmation. The gelding that the girl was leading, his confirmation was extremely good, but he had side bones on his front left. I placed your gelding last because he really does a poor job of representing the Percheron breed. The Stallion and mare cross for him didn't work the best. I'm sorry if you're disappointed, but that's why they placed so low. If you would like, I can show you what side bones are."

He showed us the side bones on Pete and explained Joe's faults, confirmation wise. After he explained and showed us everything, I was a little confused. Were Pete and Joe defective?

What should I do? They were my pride and joy! The judge went on to tell me that Pete and Joe are fine for how I use them, as long as I have no intentions of showing them at the state fair and other big shows. With a little reluctance I went over to Clyde and shook his hand after the judge left. He thanked me and suggested we hook Pete and Joe up for a six horse hitch at the next field days.

That afternoon Judy and I saddled the geldings and rode around the fair grounds. When we came back to the draft horse barn, Kelly and her parents were waiting. Kelly was dressed up like a cowgirl, hat, pink boots and all.

"Hi Kelly, how you doing?" Judy said as she got down off of Pete. Judy knelt down to Kelly's level. "You sure look nice in your cowgirl clothes! Are you ready to ride?"

I put Joe away as Becky and Judy worked with Kelly and Pete. I looked back and there was Kelly giving Pete one of her famous leg hugs. Kelly went in front of Pete. He lowered his massive head and she hugged his muzzle. Pete gently nuzzled her in between hugs. Pete and Kelly were best of buds.

"Kelly, are you ready to jump up in the saddle?" I asked while I pulled the bill of her hat.

She looked at me with the special eyes God gave her and nodded slowly. Her parents gave me the okay and soon Kelly was up in the saddle. The joy in her face was priceless. She looked back to her parents for their approval. Pete arched his neck back towards her and gave her a soft nicker.

"Kelly, hang on. We're going for a ride now," I said as I lead Pete to the barn door. Her parents and Becky were taking tons of pictures. I led Pete around about ten minutes with Kelly on his back while Kelly and Pete talked back and forth. All of a sudden Pete pushed me hard in the back with his head, almost knocking me down.

I stopped. "Pete, what is wrong? You have never done that before." I looked him in the eye and held him by his muzzle. He nickered at me and pushed me back again. "Pete, what are you trying to say, do you want to do this without me?" It's hard to believe, but it seemed Pete slowly shook his head ''yes.'' I looked at Judy and Becky and they gave me the thumbs up. I tied the reins over his neck where Kelly could reach them and slowly stepped back. Kelly hugged Pete's neck and talked to him in her special language. Pete cautiously took a few steps. Everyone started to clap as Kelly rode Pete all alone! Her parents stood there, not sure how to react. Kelly was in charge of a gentle giant. Pete and Kelly put on quite a show. They backed, turned both ways, and even trotted some. The whole time Kelly hung on to the saddle horn with the world's biggest smile.

I thanked the Lord as I stood there and watched. This was way better than a blue ribbon!

Chapter 4
"Goodbyes and College"

After the fair Becky and I worked with the geldings on Roman Driving in our spare time. We started with Becky and me standing on their backs in the barn. We would walk back and forth on each of them to get them used to a foot being in their backs. We had Becky lead them one at a time in the round pen as I would ride and work my way up to standing. Wow! Standing on an eighteen-hand horse, it seemed like I could touch the heavens. Unfortunately, it was not going all that well. I jumped off a lot because I couldn't keep my balance. Dad came by and suggested a light rope around their neck that I could hang on to. That helped tremendously, and soon I was staying up on each gelding while they trotted. This was awesome! Mom came out and took some pictures.

As we rested, Becky said, "Jude, are you going to let me give it a try?"

She caught me off guard. It never crossed my mind that she would want to try.

"Sure you can. Let me know when you're ready."

Soon Becky was going around standing on their backs like an old pro. She actually had better balance than I did. I looked up and she grinned with approval. She rode Pete first, then Joe. We both thought Joe had a smoother gait than Pete.

"Becky, I'll go get their bridles, and if you wish, you can try driving from their backs first."

"Sure."

We snapped some lead ropes into the bits to give us more length. With Becky on Joe's back hanging on to the lead ropes, I led him for a little while, then faded back. Joe wanted to stop but Becky kissed to him to keep going. I tossed my lead rope over his neck and went to the center of the pen to watch. Becky was doing great and so was Joe. She walked him and trotted him both directions, stopped and started him several times, and turned some tight circles. She drove Joe right up to me and stopped.

"Good boy, Joe, good boy!" I praised him as I rubbed his neck.

"Becky, you did great. What do you think?"

"This is sooo... neat, Jude. Wait till you do it! Atta boy, Joe, you did so good."

I took my turn with Joe and was soon driving him by myself: turning, trotting, walking, stopping, starting. We took turns with Pete and got him to the same level as Joe. The next step would be to hook them together as a team. The trick would be to keep them close enough to each other.

The next day Becky and I gave them a quick review of Roman Driving and hitched them to the hay wagon. The tugs and neck yoke would keep them close enough to allow one foot on each horse. Becky started them out driving normally with me standing on their backs. We did that for ten to twenty minutes, and then I added lead ropes to the bits. Becky could still drive if she had to, but soon I was driving them, and Becky just allowed extra slack in her lines. We went through all the motions: walking, trotting, turning, stopping, starting, and backing. I couldn't believe I was actually Roman Driving Pete and Joe. I soon learned to focus ahead of us instead of on their heads. Watching their heads lulled me into a trance and I almost fell off. Becky took her turn on their backs and did very well.

That week we Roman Drove Pete and Joe every day on the hay wagon. We all were gaining confidence with each run, and soon took our show to the road. You should have seen Mr. Olson's expression as we pulled into his drive with me standing on their backs.

"My, my, you kids have done well! How many times have you fallen off?"

"A few times in the beginning when we were working them single in the round pen." I answered.

Pete and Joe understood Roman Driving well enough to try it

without harnesses. That was the true test of both them and Becky and myself. We line-drove them a lot with bridles and collars only, no harnesses. They seemed to be staying with each other very well, so up I went to give it a try. Becky line drove them as I stood on Joe, and I gradually eased a foot over to Pete. I rigged up a two-by-two piece of wood attached to Joe's hames that I could grab hold of from a standing position. We eventually worked up to true Roman Driving, with no one line driving, and no two-by-two attached to the hames. It was truly exciting to drive them from standing on their backs. I now had a team of Percherons that were broke to ride, drive, and Roman Drive.

Judy called me one night and we set up date number five, bike riding and a picnic lunch at Sibley State Park. Sibley has many trails and hills so it was a good workout. I had a hard time keeping up with Judy, it must have been the bike. We ate lunch on a picnic table overlooking Lake Andrew. Her hair gleamed in the sunlight as a breeze gently lifted it. The more time I spent with Judy, the more time I wanted to spend with her.

"Judy, thank you, I had a good time. You know, I would like to go on date number six if that's all right with you," I said.

"Would that mean we are officially courting, Pal?"

"Yes ma'am, that's my intention. Of course I need to ask your father's permission, along with yours."

Judy asked, "What happens this fall when we go our separate ways for college?"

"Good question. I believe that is all the more reason to do this. It will be a very true test of our relationship. If we are still together after a few years, then I believe God is behind it." I continued, "If we find out we weren't meant for each other, then let's leave on a positive note."

"Wow. It was so simple in high school, but now we are both moving apart and becoming adults. It's kind of scary."

I looked into her eyes and saw uncertainty. "Judy, God always has tests for his followers. We need to trust Him and seek His guidance. Remember Romans 8:28: 'And we know that in all things God works for the good of those who love him, who have been called according to his purpose."

Summer flew by and next thing I knew, I was heading west for Bible college and Judy was going east to Crown College. It was both exciting and scary to leave home for the first time. Mom was pretty quiet as she helped pack up my stuff. It was decided that

Mom and Becky would drive out with me while Dad stayed home for chores.

I drove over to Judy's to say goodbye. She was out in the yard swinging as I pulled in. I have to admit, I had a hard time walking out to her without getting emotional. She was beautiful in my eyes with her hair billowing behind her as she swung through the cottonwood seeds in the air.

"Judy, I figured you might be out here swinging in your favorite tree."

She smiled and didn't answer back. I think I could see a few tears working their way down her cheeks. I sat down in the grass beside the swing and just let her glide back and forth. I think it was five minutes before she slowed her pace and came to a stop. She looked my way with her water-filled eyes, and as our eyes met, her tears seemed to explode even more. I had to look away, otherwise I'd be crying too.

"Judy, I want to thank you for these last seven or eight months. Getting to know the real Judy Clemons was a privilege and it's something I will never forget. God has special plans for you and it was great to see Him at work through you. My hope is we can survive this long-distance relationship and be standing at the altar together someday in God's time."

Judy was gaining her composure back as she said, "Jude, how can you talk so frankly about this? It almost seems like you really don't care."

With that, I got up and had her sit on my lap on the swing. "I think it is important for both of us to remember to place God first. I think I love you and I believe you love me. Right now we both need to go on with our future plans and see if God keeps us together. If we really weren't made for each other, I'd rather find out in college than in marriage. Dad said if I go west and find that I really don't miss you, then it probably is not meant to be, and the same for you. I do believe I will miss you tremendously."

"But Jude, you will be so far away, and my nursing program is three or four years. I don't know how I will make it." She cried on my shoulder.

I thought for a minute. "Can you remember when you were a freshman?"

"Yes, but what's that got to do with it?"

"Doesn't it seem like we were just freshmen yesterday? My point is that time goes faster than we think or like, so three or four years from now we will look back and see the same years pass quickly."

"I suppose you're right."

"Now, we can text each other and I'll be back during Thanksgiving and Christmas. So give me a hug and then I'll push you awhile. I'd like it if you would stay in the swing as I leave; that way I will have that picture in my mind of you swinging."

As she wiped her eyes she said, "Will you pray before you push me?"

"Father God, thank you for all you give us. Thank you for placing Judy in my life. Lord, please be with Judy and me as we go our separate ways. Please be with our studies and our travels. Lord, we ask that we both recognize open and closed doors and that your will be done. We pray this through your son Jesus Christ. Amen."

I hugged Judy and sat her back down on the swing. I fought back tears as I started to push her. As I pushed, I had to laugh inside as I cried outwardly. Here I was tearing up over leaving Judy Clemons! God does work in mysterious ways. I slowly made my way back to my car and never took my eye off Judy till I was to the road. I headed to Mr. Olson's to say my goodbyes.

Mr. Olson was in the house doing dishes when I got there. He kept his back to me and said, "I suppose you expect me to check in on them two nags of yours when you're gone?"

"That would be nice if you would."

"One day you're wet behind the ears and the next day you're heading off to some college somewhere. What's a man suppose to do?" He paused a couple minutes. "Now don't go getting too big for your britches when they hand you that diploma. Remember where you came from, papers don't pull a plow and I hope to pitch a few loads with ya come spring break."

"I'll look forward to that, Mr. Olson."

He seemed to struggle to find the right words to say as he stopped with the dishes. He spoke again without facing me. "There's an envelope on the table there that's yours to take, a few Bible verses and a little green stuff to get you started. It's not much but it's better than a poke in the eye with a sharp stick. Why certainly, why certainly."

"I thank you, but you didn't...."

"I've always considered you like my own son. I'm proud of ya and so are your parents. God bless, and go out there and give'em hell."

I answered back, "Why certainly, why certainly."
I slipped out the back door of his home fighting tears for the second time. This saying goodbye stuff was getting hard to handle. I slowly drove out his drive, studying every building as I went to etch them into my mind. This was like a second home to me.

When I got home there was the smell of food in the air. Mom, Dad, and Becky were just sitting down to a lunch of big juicy hamburgers. I washed up and sat down just in time for Dad to say grace. "Lord, bless this food to us and we thank you for providing. And Lord bless these goodbyes, these tears, and bless their travel out west. May we serve you humbly. Amen."

"Honey, I'll bet you didn't bring any tissues with you when you said your goodbyes," Mom said.

"Why would you think I'd need tissues?"

"Maybe it's when you walked in here with bloodshot eyes and a sleeve that's all wet. Your mother has seen that before."

"Yeah, you're right. Between Mr. Olson and Judy, I shed more tears today than I thought I would."

Dad said, "Praise God. Just think if you weren't going to miss Judy and Mr. Olson."

After lunch it was time to say goodbye to Pete and Joe, so I grabbed a couple apples and the curry comb and headed to the pasture. The air had a hint of fall in it as I walked towards Pete and Joe. They were play fighting as I walked closer, biting each other's flanks, rearing up, and throwing soft kicks at each other. I stood there as they circled me, pretending to ignore me.

"Pete, Joe, you big dummies! Get in here before I decide not to give you these apples."

With that said, they decided to turn it into a game of chicken with me. They would run away and turn and come running straight at me, full blast. They were hoping I'd get spooked or something. I'd whistle just as they were closing in and they would stop in their tracks and stare at me with their nostrils flaring, spin around, fart as they kicked in the air and start all over again. They did three or four rounds of that as I stood my ground. I decided to pretend to just walk away and ignore them. Yes sir, it worked. Soon they were following me like two lost puppies. They would give me a low nicker and nudge me in the back as they tagged along.

"Okay, you knuckleheads, I guess you can have your apples."

They each took an apple out of my hand and munched it down as I started currying them. I curried their bellies, necks, tail heads and chests as they stood there soaking it all in. "You guys are pretty special and I'm going to miss ya a ton. You make sure you listen to Becky while I'm gone, ya hear?" They nudged me with their massive heads.

Next thing I knew, they each had their head on my shoulders as I rubbed their ears. It's funny how much weight they bared down on me as I stood there.

"Ya know, it wasn't that long ago I was bottle feeding you rascals. Now look at ya. You're each as big as a house. Thank you for all the good times. Pete, are you gonna give me a ride back up to the house?"

I jumped on his back and rode up to the pasture gate with Joe tagging along trying to bite Pete in the rump. I got down and gave them each a big hug and took one last smell of their hides, then chased them off in fun. They high-tailed it back to where we came from as I headed to the barn to say goodbye to Dad.

"I'm sorry I can't ride out with you this time," Dad said.

"That's fine, Dad. I understand. I sure didn't think it would be this hard to leave, Dad."

"That's very normal. Look at all you have here that you have to leave. God never promised a life without strife. So it's up to you what you will do. Mom and I have confidence in you and Becky, so stand tall and pray at all times and you'll do great."

"But…"

"Jude, be very careful who you listen to! Satan is trying to convince you to just do nothing. You're not the first kid to be going off to college. Look at the opportunities the good Lord is heading your way. Remember, God is in control. Make sure it is his will and not yours."

"You're right, Dad, but it's definitely harder now with Judy in the picture. I never would have thought she would be a reason to stay home."

"Let's pray so we can get you on your way," Dad said.

Dad prayed over me and I headed to the car. I had packed it earlier that morning. Mom and Becky were all smiles as they loaded up with me to head west. I think they were looking forward to this trip, one of those mother-daughter things.

It wasn't till then I realized I hadn't said goodbye to Fuzz! She was with Becky all morning so I had lost track of her. She sat there staring at me with her little beady eyes. "Fuzz, you old rascal you, what am I going to do without you?" I reached down and picked her up. "Now you take care of Pete and Joe while I'm gone." I rubbed on her ears as she leaned into my hand, trying to absorb as much as she could. I started to tear up as I held her. She started licking my face. I think she knew something was different. "Fuzz, ol' girl, you're my best friend and I'm going to miss ya big time. You and Dad take care of each other while I'm gone."

Dad said another prayer just before we all left. I slowly pulled out the drive as Pete and Joe ran alongside the driveway. This was their way of saying goodbye. Our drive west went fine and soon we were in Colorado. Mom, Becky and I unloaded the van and they helped me set up my dorm room. We checked into the administration office and found out when and where orientation would be.

With all the preliminary items done, Mom took us out to supper before she left to head back home with Becky. I sat there across from Becky and Mom thinking how lucky I was to have a family like I did. I was sure I would miss them greatly, but I was also looking forward to this next chapter in my life. This would be my first time away from Mom and Dad except for Bible camps and stay overs at friends. Yes, it was my first time of independence, and I truly thought I was ready for it, thanks to God and the support of my family.

We drove back to my dorm room and started the process of saying goodbye to Mom and Becky. Mom started in, "Honey, now you make sure you get enough sleep, and are you sure you know how to wash your clothes? What about meals and…"

"Mom, yes, yes and yes. I'll be fine. Now you and Becky enjoy your girl time with each other as you drive home and don't worry about me. What does the Good Book say about worrying?"

"Oh, I'm sorry, Jude, but you're my first kid to leave!" Mom exclaimed.

I laughed. "You just watch, I'll probably come home for Thanksgiving dinner and bring the whole dinner with me. Honey-glazed ham, sweet potato pie, green bean casserole …"

"Okay, young man, Becky and I both heard you. Remember to cook enough for Granny and Gramps and Mr. Olson! Now give me a hug so we can get going."

I gave Mom a big hug and thanked her for all that she had done for me. I fought back tears the whole time. Mom quietly slipped into the car so I could say goodbye to Becky.

"Jude, ya know I'm going to miss ya. Thanks for being a big brother. Ya know, I have to admit, I'm looking forward to taking care of Pete and Joe for you."

"I'm sure Pete and Joe will be very well cared for while I'm gone. Just don't spoil them too bad, otherwise they won't listen to me when I get back."

"You study hard and make sure you call Mom and Dad every once in awhile," she said as she fought off tears. "Give me a hug before I totally lose it!"

I stood there as Mom and Becky pulled out of the parking lot. I believe we were all crying.

Chapter 5
"College Life and Beyond"

Yes sir, college life was very different from high school. Classes were much more difficult than I expected and attendance wasn't really a requirement. To a certain degree, the professors didn't care if their students were in class or not. It seems all I did was study, cook meals, and do laundry. It took me a while, but I finally got organized and used to the new life-style, so it was less hectic.

My roommate, Wade Estep, and I got along pretty well. He was one of those guys that had zero body fat on him and could stay in shape without really doing much exercise. We had several of the same classes, so that helped with some of the studies. He was from a small town in Ohio and was an avid bow hunter. He couldn't believe that I didn't hunt. Since he was so far from home I talked him into coming home with me for Thanksgiving. He had not been raised on a farm, so he was looking forward to a country-style Thanksgiving.

Judy and I had decided to wait a full week before I called her so we could both get settled in to our new surroundings. I was a little nervous as I dialed the phone that Saturday night.

"Hello?"

Just to hear her "hello" was wonderful. "Judy, how are you doing?"

"I'm fine, but I miss you a lot. The one blessing is I'm so busy with studies that I have little time to myself."

"Is now a good time to talk?"

"Why certainly, why certainly," she said, laughing.

"Ya know, Judy, I miss you more than I thought I would. I can't wait to see ya during Thanksgiving break."

"I can't wait either."

"How are studies going for that future nurse?"

"It's too early to say, but I think okay. I think I like what I've chosen to study and I've talked with some second-year students and they say it's hard, but worth it."

"Judy, that is so good to hear. I'm sure you'll make a fine nurse. Ya know I miss you and Mom and Dad and Becky, but I can't believe how much I think of Ol' Fuzz and the geldings. My roommate will be spending Thanksgiving at our place this year. He's from Ohio so he wasn't going to go home that far. He's a pretty good kid. I'm blessed to have him for a roommate."

"Jude, I miss you and I'd love to talk all night but I have a biology test Monday that needs some attention, so I'll have to let you go, okay?"

"Why certainly, why certainly. Bye, Judy, and God bless."

"Bye, Jude. Take care."

Before we knew it our first eight weeks of college were over and Wade and I were packed up in his car headed for home. The trip home went fast between Wade telling of his youth in Ohio and my stories of youth in Minnesota. We soon pulled into the driveway. Pete and Joe were out in the pasture and Ol' Fuzz came running out the back door lickety-split.

I hollered, "Fuzz, you little mutt!" as she ran our way. I picked her up and she started licking my face. She was going crazy. Mom said she would lay on my bed and whine at times.

"Fuzz, yes, I missed you too." I gave her a big hug and roughed her up a little and put her down. Yes sir, Ol' Fuzz took off in her big circles running as fast as her little legs would allow. She darted in and out between Wade and me huffing and puffing. We chased her and clapped and that made her all the more crazy. Next thing we knew, Pete and Joe whinnied and headed our way at a full gallop. Of course, Fuzz thought she needed to dart in between them as they thundered through the pasture towards us. It was a sight to see, eight pounding hooves with one scruffy dog zipping between them. It's a wonder she didn't get trampled.

I ran over to the fence to greet Pete and Joe. They just stood there, ears and eyes all perked up and ready for action. I jumped the fence and gave each one a big hug. They each snorted and

Joe put his nose next to mine so I could blow into it. I scratched each of their bellies and then shooed them away, knowing they'd put on a show. Sure enough, they spun, kicked, and farted as they trotted away. I whistled and they pranced all the more, since they had an audience in Wade and needed to show him their stuff. They would circle back and let me rub on them and then spin and dart off. I decided to ignore them the next time they came back. I turned my back on them and stood there in silence. It wasn't long before they came thundering up to me, and I thought, "Are they going to stop in time?" I stood there dead quiet, looking the other way. I could hear their breathing right behind me, and soon I could feel their breaths on the back of my neck. I had a hard time not laughing at the big dummies as they stood right on my heels. I should have known what was next. They each nudged with their massive heads and pushed me forward. Then they draped their heads over my shoulder and lightly snorted. How could a guy ignore that?

"You big, lazy dummies, what am I to do with you?" I asked as I stroked their faces.

"Joe, you gonna give me a ride?" I grabbed some mane hair and swung up on his back. I gave him a neck hug and kissed for him to go. "Easy, Joe, easy, Joe, I have no bridle or saddle." I rode him up to the barn and back and then slid off his rump for a perfect landing.

By now Mom, Dad and Becky were down by the fence. I made the proper introduction of Wade to all of them and we headed to unload the car. As we walked, Mom stated, "Wade, I'm sure glad you could come and you're welcome anytime. I want you to know that if you need something, don't be shy. Is that understood?"

"Yes, ma'am."

It was near chore time, so Wade and I changed clothes so we could help Dad. Wade had never been on a dairy farm before, so it was kind of funny to watch him. He couldn't believe you could get that close to a cow without getting kicked or run over. By the end of milking, Dad had him washing cows ahead of the milkers. I think Wade really liked what he was doing. Ol' Fuzz stuck by me like glue as I did the calf and young stock chores. Wade went up with me while I climbed the silo chute to lower the unloader. He was full of questions, so I explained that you have to change the chute to the next door as the silo gets emptied.

Dad was finished with cleaning the milkers when we got back

from adjusting the silo unloader. We shut up the barn and headed into the house for some of Mom's home cooking. It wasn't until I sank my teeth into that tender pork roast that I realized how much better her food was than cafeteria food at college. Wade and I put down our fair share of home cooking that night. To top it off, Mom surprised us with lemon pie.

As we ate our pie. Dad asked, "Wade, tell us about Ohio, your parents, and your ambitions, if you don't mind."

"Sure I can, no problem, Mr. Bonner. Before I start, I want to thank your family for allowing me to stay here over Thanksgiving, and Mrs. Bonner, that was one of the best meals I've ever had. I'm curious to find out how great Thanksgiving dinner will be after this feast."

Mom replied, "You're more than welcome. I'm glad you liked it."

"Well, I was raised in Monclova, Ohio and went to Anthony Wayne High School in Whitehouse, Ohio. I have three older brothers and Dad and Mother back home. Dad is a dentist and Mother mainly worked at home raising us boys. She also did a lot of volunteer work. I like to tinker with engines and hope to attend mechanics school after this year of Bible college. I hope to marry a Christian gal someday and raise a family. So that is my story. And thank you for allowing me to milk with you tonight. I'd like to get up in the morning and help again if that's okay."

Dad laughed. "It's up to you, Wade. Five-thirty comes pretty early and the pay isn't all that great."

"Five-thirty it is, sir. I'll be there."

The five of us played cards till eleven o'clock that night. Laughing, telling stories and eating popcorn kept us going. Finally, Wade and I admitted we were very tired. As I headed to bed I asked, "Are you sure you want to get up for chores in the morning?"

"Sure, I didn't come all this way just to sleep."

I had to laugh a little. "You're our guest, so whatever you wish."

It was wonderful to sleep in my own bed again with the familiar smells, the covers, my old pillow and, of course, Fuzz. Chores came awful early that next morning, but I thought Wade was right in his philosophy. When exposed to something new, don't sleep through it, engage in it and learn the most you can.

Mom had waffles waiting for us after chores. I do believe

Wade and I set a record for how many we ate that morning. "My goodness boys, how can you eat so much?" Mom asked.

"Jude, what are your plans for the rest of today?" Dad asked. "Wade and I were going to hitch the geldings and run over to Mr. Olson's place and then maybe get a load of wood. Or do you need help with something else?"

"No, that's fine. How about you do chores tonight so I can take your lovely mother to the movies?"

"Sure, Wade and I can handle that. After chores Judy might come over to hang out. Is that okay?"

"That's fine, son."

Wade and I got the geldings in the barn and I showed Wade how to harness a draft horse. I had to laugh. He had straps crisscrossed and upside down. It was his first time standing that close to a big draft horse. He went real slow and gave them lots of room around their back legs, thinking they would kick.

"They won't kick you, Wade. You can brush right up against them."

"No way am I going to trust them big brutes. First you guys tell me cows won't kick and now horses! Look at the size of the feet on them boys. Back at school when you talked of Pete and Joe and how big they were, well, I guess I just didn't believe it. Standing between them now, I have to admit these guys are pretty awesome creatures."

I drove them out of the barn and hooked them to the hay wagon. Becky came out and rode with us. I think she had more than horses on her mind. Pete and Joe were very spunky, since they hadn't been hitched since before I went to school. Our trip to Mr. Olson's didn't take long. We hobbled Pete and Joe when we got there while Mr. Olson came out of the house. He gave Wade the grand tour of his farm. Of course he had to bring Molly and Ladd into the barn to show them off. He saved the wagon and harness for last. Yes sir, Mr. Olson was all smiles when showing off Molly, Ladd, the wagon, and the harness.

He started laughing. "Wade, that there wagon and harness will be used for my neighbor kid's wedding pretty soon. Yes sir, that's when I charge him big money. Why certainly, why certainly." I don't think Wade knew he was talking about me and Judy. Mr. Olson asked him, "What do you think a man should pay for such fine equipment?"

"Geez, sir, I don't really know. I've never been around

anything like this before."

Mr. Olson continued, "Never been around something like this, hey? I have to assume you'll be invited for that special day."

"I don't think so, Mr. Olson. I don't know any neighbors of yours that are getting married."

Mr. Olson laughed again. "Oh, I thought you knew that neighbor. Sorry."

We left Mr. Olson's and headed home to load up chainsaws and stuff for getting firewood. As I pulled in the driveway, I saw Judy's car parked by the house. She wasn't supposed to be home till the afternoon. I drove Pete and Joe up by the house and ran in to see where Judy was. There she sat talking with Mom at the breakfast table. She looked my way and did a quick wave and kept right on talking. I sat down across the room and gazed at her. She was even prettier than I remembered: her hair, her eyes, her cheek bones. I sat there quietly. She would look my way and smile every once in a while. It meant a lot to me that she was so close with Mom. It wasn't long before Becky joined in with them, chatting and ignoring me. I finally took the hint and slipped out the back door to get some wood with Wade and the geldings.

As we drove toward the woods, Wade asked, "What neighbor kid was Mr. Olson talking about? I didn't understand why he thought I would be invited to a total stranger's wedding."

I answered back confidently, "I would guess you have a good chance of being invited. Not sure how soon that wedding might happen but you'll probably be there."

He looked at me questioningly so I added. "After being your roommate this year, I hope you don't consider me a total stranger."

Wade raised his eyebrows. "You? You didn't mention you were getting married."

I shrugged. "Well, not yet. I haven't asked her yet. I'm pretty sure Judy is the one." We both laughed at how long it had taken Wade to figure it out.

Wade and I had enough time to get two loads of wood before chores. It was funny to see Wade around Pete and Joe and chainsaws. He grew up in a small town and was never around this type of stuff before. Wade helped unharness Pete and Joe and curry them down. I even talked him into picking up a foot on Pete, which he thought was awesome.

It was now chore time. Wade wanted to know about everything

I did, including setting up the milk house, hauling milkers, wash water and towels down to the end of the barn. By now he was gaining confidence and was a really big help. Judy and Becky came out and talked with us for a while. Then they ran into town to rent a movie for after chores and got a few things for supper. Wade and I finished chores and headed into the house to see what Becky and Judy had fixed for supper. We could smell bacon as soon as we stepped in the back door. Becky was frying up big cheeseburgers, while Judy had spinach salads in the works. Judy put me to work right away cutting big slabs of onion and tomatoes for the burgers. Now those burgers were on the serious side of life; bacon, onion, lettuce, tomato, cheese, and mayo. Add baked beans with extra brown sugar and the taste buds were doing cartwheels.

After we ate, we watched a movie and played cards till two in the morning. I hadn't stayed up that late in a long time. The card game was pretty competitive. Becky and Judy played against Wade and me, and you guessed it, they cleaned up on us big time.

Next day was Thanksgiving Day. I slept in a little, but Wade had gotten up and helped Dad with chores. Mom and Becky were slaving away when I got up and the aroma from their cooking was all through the house. Wade and Dad came in and soon we were all sitting down having dinner with Granny, Gramps, and Mr. Olson. Yes sir, I think Wade would remember this country Thanksgiving for many years. In fact, I was starting to wonder if he and Becky were becoming more than friends.

Wade and I drove back to college the Sunday after Thanksgiving. A couple of days later my phone rang and it was Dad. It was odd that he called so soon after we just left.

"Hello?"

"Jude, do you have a few minutes?"

"Sure Dad, what's up?"

"It's Fuzz. She has limped ever since you headed back to college. I've felt her pads and feet for any slivers or thorns and found nothing. Not sure if she maybe got stepped on by a cow or the geldings?"

"Have you checked her temperature?"

"Yes, and that was okay."

I justified in my mind that she would be okay. "She probably just sprained it or something."

"Your mother and I will keep an eye on her. I think half of it is she misses you. We'll talk next week. Goodbye son."

I hung up the phone and stood there awhile not knowing what to think. I wish I could have driven back home and fixed my best friend. Except for the episode with Herbie, Fuzz has always been in great shape. She was now ten years old, but should live to be around fifteen. Mom called a week after Dad had, and Fuzz was no better. Mom stated that Fuzz would yip in pain every once in awhile as she walked. Mom was pretty concerned and talked of taking her to the veterinarian to see what she thinks.

Between school, Fuzz, and Judy, my mind was full. School took the most effort, as you can imagine. A one-year bible school to take in the Old and New Testament is a full load. When I got caught up with my studies, I would spend time with Judy on the phone late at night. It's hard to explain, but just to hear her voice was so special. I think I was falling in love. We could kill forty five minutes on the phone with ease. She would always ask how Fuzz was doing, and Pete and Joe.

I was starting to dread the phone ringing from Mom or Dad. With each call Fuzz seemed to be getting worse. It was a cold, snowy night about a week before I was going home for Christmas break when they called again. "Jude, your Dad is on the phone with us, can you talk?"

"Yes, what's going on with Fuzz?"

There was silence at their end for a few moments. "Fuzz's limp has been getting worse, so we took her in to get checked." Another long pause, I slowly sat down.

My lip quivered. "What did the vet say?"

Dad spoke, "She has a mass on the bone of her left front leg. The vet is strongly assuming it is cancer."

I was stunned! "What can be done about it? Can't they just cut it out?"

"Jude, it's not that simple. First, treatment is very expensive, second they assume the cancer has spread, and at her age, amputation would be too hard on her."

I was losing it at my end and the tears were on their way. "There has to be something that can be done, isn't there?"

Mom slowly said, "Jude, you can let nature take its course, or you can end her pain before it gets worse."

"No way!" I sobbed into the phone. "Mom and Dad, you don't understand."

I held the phone down by my side as I tried to get myself back together. I tried to talk a couple times but just couldn't. A few minutes went past before I was able to talk again. "Will she be okay till I get home for Christmas?"

"We think so Honey, but you need to decide what you want to do soon." Mom said.

Dad hesitantly said. "Jude, did you want us to do something before you get home?"

I let out a big gasp of air. "No, this is something I need to do."

That last week of school dragged on like it was never going to end. Finally Wade and I were heading home for Christmas. While driving, I was thinking neither Wade or I were going back for a real Christmas. Wade was coming home with me instead of going to his family for Christmas. I think Becky was the reason. And I really wasn't going home for Christmas as much as I was going home to take care of Fuzz.

Wade and I did a lot of talking on the drive home, so he asked me, "Jude, as Becky's brother, do you have any reason why she shouldn't hang around me?"

I smiled. "So that explains why you're heading to Minnesota for Christmas instead of Ohio." His face turned red. "Wade, no, I don't. Becky is a great sister and I think a lot of you too. Ya know you need to ask Dad."

"Yes, yes, I know. I plan to help with chores and ask him then."

I laughed. "Maybe it's your wedding that I'll be going to first."

As we pulled into our driveway I was scared to death of what Fuzz might look like. Dad was doing chores as we pulled in, so Wade went to the barn as I headed toward the house. I slipped in the back door and put my clothes bag down and took my shoes off. I walked into the living room and Fuzz lay beside Becky, sound asleep on her dog mat. Becky gave me a hug and quietly left the room so I could be alone with Fuzz. I slowly laid beside Fuzz and put my hand on her little body. She raised her head slightly and whimpered softly. I could tell she had lost muscle tone as I softly rubbed her. I pulled her close to me and held her as I wept. She gradually got up on her good front leg, turned, and started licking my face. She didn't put any weight on her bad leg. It just hung there all swollen up.

"Fuzz, do you know how special you are? I'm so sorry you are hurting, girl. What can I get for you? How about I sneak you one of Mom's cookies?" She had a different look in her eyes, one I'd never seen before. Fuzz got up and hobbled over to the kitchen with me. I gave her a cookie and she scooted back to her dog mat and lay there with her cookie in front of her. I scooped her up with her cookie and sat in the easy chair with Fuzz on my lap. She would look up at me and then lay her head down again as I stroked her ears gently. I was slowly saying my goodbyes to my best friend as I sat there crying. "Fuzz you scruffy little mutt, what am I going to do without you? Who's going to help me with gophers? Who's going to keep the cats in line and help Dad get cows in the stanchions? I remember when we brought you home, you were just a walking fuzz ball. You were even fat! You used to chew on my fingers and shred anything we left laying around, including Mother's garden hose. That cost me some dish time you mangy mutt."

Mom, Dad, and Wade came in from chores. Mom sat with me while the guys cleaned up.

"I'm sorry that you have to go through this, Jude, especially at Christmas. She's been with you on all of your adventures, a very loyal friend."

"Mom, I know I have to put her down, but I've never done that before. I'm not sure if I can do it by myself."

"I think I know what you mean. Maybe Becky would go with you? She has grown very close to Fuzz after you left for college."

Becky came back down to join us and soon Dad and Wade sat down with us. It was a pretty somber crowd. I broke the silence with a story about Fuzz that was in the back of my mind.

"I'll never forget the time Perry and Harold were staying overnight, sleeping on the floor. Of course Fuzz had to sleep with Harold, like he couldn't sleep without her. As Harold lay there, he was jawing at Perry. Perry had enough, so he started to sneak over to attack Harold in the dark. The room fell dead silent as we all knew Perry was stalking toward Harold. Next thing we heard was a low growl. For some reason, Perry turned around immediately. No one was going to interrupt Fuzz's sleep!"

"I think I remember that night." Mom laughed.

"How about the time rat hunting with Harold and Perry and we came back to get Fuzz so she could get a rat out of the cab of Harold's old truck. Harold and Perry couldn't believe how quick she was. That same night she saved my life when Herbie decided to try to kill me!"

"Who is Herbie?" Wade asked.

"Herbie was our bull at the time and was charging Jude, until ol' Fuzz came to his rescue." Dad answered. "Yes sir, Fuzz was one tough customer."

"Mom, do you want to know how many of your fresh baked cookies were shared with Fuzz over the years?" I laughed.

"I'm sure more than I'll ever know." Mom yawned.

It was getting late, so Mom and Becky headed to bed after saying their goodnights. They even stopped and rubbed Fuzz's ears.

"Dad, what are your thoughts for Fuzz?"

He shook his head slowly. "It should happen soon, and the best place is at the vet clinic. I'll pay the bill, but I think you need to take her in. Fuzz was mainly your dog and that's part of the deal."

"I guess you're right, Dad. I'll call them in the morning."

It was getting late so we decided to head to bed. I looked down and noticed Fuzz still hadn't eaten her cookie. I carefully got up with Fuzz in my arms and carried her upstairs. I laid her on my bed as I got Wade set up with covers and brushed my teeth. I got back to bed and Fuzz had not moved. She must have been hurting bad! I put her up by my pillow and slid in beside her. This was the last time of sharing my bed with Ol Fuzz. I lay there thinking of the next day and how that would pan out. My mind went from one thing to the next. Sleep was scarcer than hen's teeth that night.

At breakfast, Becky asked if she could go with me. I was glad she was willing. I asked Mom to call and schedule an appointment with the vet while I took Fuzz on a last tour of our farm. I put my winter coat on and cradled Fuzz in my arms as I walked out the back door. It was bitterly cold with a strong wind from the northwest and the snow crunched with each step I took.

Fuzz and I started with the chickens first. I don't think she ever did like the chickens. We stopped at the cats in the barn, then the cows, and from there we went to the hogs. "Fuzz, do you think them hogs will ever forgive you for all the times you tormented them and made their lives miserable?"

Pete and Joe were last. Fuzz was getting cold, so I tucked her into my jacket. As I walked toward their pasture, Pete and Joe came running up to greet us. When they got to the fence they stretched their massive heads over the hot fence and sniffed at Fuzz. They both backed a few steps and snorted softly. Joe reached back over and ran his top lip over Fuzz's head and ear.

Fuzz perked up a little and looked up at me. I truly think the geldings knew something was different. Could they smell the cancer on her breath? Pete stood back and pawed at the ground, almost as if to invite Fuzz for one last romp with him. "Pete and Joe, Fuzz can't come out and play, so you need to say your goodbyes." The tears froze to my face as Pete and Joe softly nickered to Fuzz. Fuzz and I were super cold, so I headed back to the house. Pete and Joe whinnied as they ran along the fence beside us.

I put Fuzz back in the house on her dog bed and got some warmer clothes on. I had to dig a hole for her final resting place. I grabbed the pick ax and safety glasses from the shop and headed out to the back pine grove. I looked for a good spot that I thought Fuzz would like and started swinging. Thirty-below winters can sure freeze ground plenty hard. Each swing brought a spray of frozen gravel chips up into my safety glasses. I would take five swings and move to another side and take another five swings. The progress was slow, but I was gradually getting closer to China.

I took a break and wiped the sweat from my brow. I noticed sun dogs left and right of the sun. God's artwork is amazing. I continued my assault on the frozen ground, my grip getting weaker with each blow. I took my gloves off as my hands were soaking wet with sweat. It wasn't long before the blisters graced me with their presence.

"God, please give me the strength I need to do this for Fuzz," I prayed as I was getting worn out and my hands were bleeding. I started singing praise songs in rhythm to the swinging of the pick ax. With God's help I was soon done with her grave.

I put my tools away and headed in to get Fuzz and Becky. Mom and Dad were waiting for me in the kitchen. Fuzz was on Dad's lap.

"Jude, you better buy one or two bags of potting soil to put over her. I also made a simple casket you can use if you wish. It's in the back of the pickup."

Mom and Dad each gave Fuzz a big hug and handed her to Becky while fighting back tears. The trip to the vet was very quiet. Fuzz sat on Becky's lap as I drove. I thought I was doing okay emotionally and thought it was all behind me. We were just about there when I looked over at Becky. She was wiping both eyes with her sleeves. Soon I followed suit. We both sat in the parking lot trying to get our composure as the windows on the truck started to steam up.

"You're going to have to do all the talking in there." Becky mumbled very quietly.

"Do you want to carry her in or should I?" I asked.

"If it's alright with you, I would like to carry her." Becky sobbed.

I checked my mirror to see how bad my eyes were, then got out and opened Becky's door. The nerve it took to walk through that clinic's door was unbearable. Becky and I stepped in and headed to the front desk.

"Do you have an appointment?" The lady behind the counter asked.

I leaned on the counter with my head down and couldn't even speak. I tried to look up at her to give her an answer but it just wasn't going to happen.

The receptionist broke the silence. "Is this appointment for Fuzz?"

Becky immediately broke away and sat down in a chair off to the side with Fuzz in her arms. I still couldn't speak, so I just nodded my head as I fought back tears.

"You can be seated over there and we will call you when the room is ready, Mr. Bonner."

I sat by Becky and Fuzz for what seemed like an eternity. Fuzz looked up at us every once in awhile.

"Becky, can I carry her into the room?"

Becky barely nodded her head while wiping more tears. The lady brought us some tissues and asked us to weigh Fuzz. I sat there not knowing what to say or do next. My body was numb with fear.

"Mr. Bonner, you can bring Fuzz in now."

Wow, was I going to be man enough to walk Fuzz through that door? I shook my head as I stood up and picked Fuzz up off Becky's lap. My vision was all blurry from tears as Becky, Fuzz and I entered the exam room. The smell of medicine and cleaner hung in the air.

Doc Strand explained the procedure they would do and gave us the option to leave or stay with Fuzz as she went. She gave us a small slip of paper and suggested we read it. She asked if we had any questions and said she would be back to check on us.

There was a poem on the paper titled ''A Dog's Plea.'' Becky slowly read it in between sobs while I held Fuzz. I never used so many tissues before in my life! The plea was as if a dog is asking for a humane death without any heroic efforts to prolong its life when the time comes. I gently hugged and kissed Fuzz. "Fuzz, you were the best! I'm going to miss you so much. I'm so sorry, I'm so sorry!" I gave her one last hug and passed her to Becky.

There was a soft knock on the door and Doc Strand stepped in followed by a vet tech. "Is it okay to proceed Jude, Becky?" Becky and I both nodded our heads without making eye contact.

"Can you please put her on the exam table? Now we are going to slip a small needle into her good front leg and she will slowly fade away. She will not be in any pain. Are you ready?"

We both nodded. I kneeled down to be at her eye level and held her bad leg while Becky had her hand on Fuzz's chest. Fuzz lay there staring at me as they slipped the IV into her leg. Her eyes never left mine, as if to say, "I'm hurting, please let me go." She slowly looked up at Becky and then back to me for a few seconds, laid her head on my hand and closed her eyes for the last time.

Chapter 6
"The Minnesota Blizzard"

With the passing of Fuzz, I had a hard time that Christmas. Fuzz was my best friend. Every place I went I expected Fuzz to be there. I hitched Pete and Joe and cut wood for Dad, which seemed to be my therapy. Mom had to talk me into going with her to find a gift for Judy. I just didn't have gifts on my mind. We found a nice necklace and earring set. Judy was swamped with homework over the Christmas break, so we didn't spend much time together. One thinks that Christmas should always be special. That Christmas was special for what seemed all the wrong reasons.

Wade and I were heading back to college again. We both studied hard those next couple months, and soon our one year of Bible school was over. As we packed our belongings, I realized that even though it seemed like only yesterday since I had met Wade, he had now become my best friend.

"Ya know, I'm coming up there this summer to see you and the family," Wade said.

I laughed. "Yeah, right. You're coming up to see Becky. You could care less about seeing me and the family."

Wade blushed. "Between your mother's home cooking and Becky, it's a pretty easy decision."

I hugged Wade. "Brother, you know you're welcome anytime. Take care and God bless."

"God bless you, too."

God had been good to me. I had a one-year Bible certificate on the shelf. I had a great family, and I was thankful for Judy, Pete, and Joe. I was living back home that summer and got a job driving a dump truck for a gravel pit. Judy was home for the summer and worked at the Belgrade Nursing Home. We spent more and more time with each other. We rode Pete and Joe many miles that summer in our spare time. Harold and Perry had come home with female friends also, so we'd get together with them.

That fall I started an eight-week course on natural hoof trimming in southern Iowa. Judy was back for her second year of nursing school. If things went well, I'd be a certified natural hoof trimmer for horses.

There was a lot more book time in trimming school than I thought there would be. There were twenty people in the course and three instructors. Some of the horses we worked on were in rough shape. Some were foundered, had huge cracks in the side walls, or had major flaring or frog fungus. It was hard work to keep up with all the stuff they were teaching us, but that made the time go by much faster. By mid-December I had passed and was heading home with another certificate in my hand.

During my windshield time, all I could think of was Judy and our future. In my opinion, Judy and I had survived our long distance separation and I think God was giving us the open door. I was a little concerned about how Judy's upbringing might affect her as she got older. I dreamed of what the wedding might be and who would be there, spring or winter time. I even thought of kids and how that might be. I really enjoyed running all these scenarios through my mind. It gave me confidence.

After settling in back home, I got a job working from three am till eight weekday mornings at a delivery company loading trucks. With this schedule I was able to gradually build up my trimming business from late morning to evening. There were many long days of hard work, but God never said life would be easy. I did a little advertising, and by word of mouth I gained more and more clients each month. Between loading trucks and trimming feet, I was gaining muscle mass also. I was feeling pretty strong and sure of myself, so I figured it was time to arm wrestle with Dad.

"So, ya think you can take the old man in an arm wrestle?" Dad chuckled as I stepped into the dining room after my shower. How did he know I was thinking of that?

"Well, ya better pack a lunch!" he said, laughing.

"How did you know I was thinking about an arm wrestle?"

"Most boys who get as strong as you need to test the waters, yes sir. Now you have to remember I'm just an old fart way past his prime, so don't be too hard on me."

So there we were, Dad on one side and me on the other side of the kitchen table. When Dad took his outer shirt off and stood there with his massive arms, I had second thoughts. We squared up our arms and shoulders to each other and with Mom and Becky watching, the test began.

Wow! Dad took me a third of the way down before I knew it. I struggled to hang on and keep my composure and I looked him in the eye as he sat there like this was a walk in the park. I started huffing and puffing and brought my arm back up to the vertical position. Becky and Mom sat there in silence. Our arms stayed vertical for a little while and then, much to my amazement, I gained a little ground. I looked over at Dad and he was now straining. We stalled arms at that point for what seemed an eternity. Gradually the arms started moving again. The only problem was they were going in the wrong direction. Dad's biceps looked like they would explode as he slowly lowered my arm to the table. Ouch, my arm felt like it was going to fall off!

"Bud Bonner, you could have at least let him win," Mom hollered.

"No, Mom, it's best this way. You and Dad taught us not to take handouts when we were young and I don't want them now," I said, rubbing my arm.

Dad sat there with a smile as he rubbed his shoulder. "Yes sir, ya don't send a boy to do a man's job."

I really did think I was going to win. Maybe next time.

We were getting an old-fashioned Minnesota winter that year with lots of snow, cold, and wind. Dad noticed the cattle getting goofy, which they usually do before a big storm. Sure enough, on the news that night the weather forecasters were predicting a blizzard in one or two days. Dad and I checked all the barn doors and made sure the generator was in working order, because we would need it to milk the cows if the power went out. Mom and Becky made a grocery run, and we seemed ready for whatever the storm would bring.

I called Mr. Olson and checked on him.

"Hello?"

"Mr. Olson, it's Jude. Are you ready for the storm?"

There was a long hesitation. "Jude, I have a bad feeling about this one. I'm a little under the weather, but I'll be fine as long as it's not too bad. I'm going to bed early and I should feel better in the morning. Good night."

As I hung up the phone, I felt like something just wasn't right.

"Mom!"

"Yes, Jude."

"I just talked with Mr. Olson and something seems to be bothering him. He said he didn't feel the best and was going to bed early."

"Jude, it won't be the first time Mr. Olson has been under the weather. He'll be fine."

"No, Mom, this was different. I swear I could hear him say 'help me' without saying it. I think I need to go over there and check on him."

"Maybe you're right. Ya better take your winter clothes just in case. This storm is supposed to hit any time."

I called him back and told him I was coming over to check on him. Mom helped me pack my things and out the door I went.

"You call us when you get there," Mom hollered as I went out the door.

"Yep."

Mr. Olson was heading to bed as I walked in the door. He seemed pretty shaky and pale.

"Mr. Olson, I'll stay here tonight and I can do chores in the morning for you while you get some rest."

"Why Jude, that isn't necessary. I shouldn't be such a burden, but I just feel off."

Mr. Olson had never missed chores from being sick, so he must have felt extra bad to agree with me. The blizzard hit that night, wind howling, snow flying horizontal, and even a few cracks of thunder. I woke at five and looked out the window. It was worse than I had expected. I'll bet we had fifteen inches of new snow on the ground and it was still snowing heavily. The wind blew right through me as I headed to the barn for chores, and the snowflakes stung my face as I walked. The outside thermometer showed ten degrees. Chores went pretty well, though I had a couple of frozen drinking cups to thaw and I had to shovel my way to feed Ladd and Molly. I was a little concerned that Mr. Olson didn't show up at some time to help.

As I stepped out the milk house door to head inside, I couldn't believe it. I could barely see the house! It had snowed four more inches during chores, and the wind was even stronger. I zipped up my chore coat, pulled my hat on tight, and headed toward the house. I was amazed how deep the snow was. I had to lean into the wind just to keep from blowing over. At one point, I honestly wondered if I was going to make it to the house. But praise God, I made it, and I hung onto the screen door super tight so the wind wouldn't rip it off the hinges as I opened it.

I quietly took off my outer chore clothes and went to check on Mr. Olson. I could hear his labored breathing as I opened his door. "Mr. Olson, I'm coming in." The door creaked as it opened. "How you doing?"

"Jude, I don't know. I've never felt this way before. It feels like a ton of bricks are on my chest and I'm all sweaty." He took a couple deep breaths. "Did chores go okay?"

"They went fine. Now I'm calling Mom to see what she has to say."

"Hello?"

"Mom, Mr. Olson is looking pretty tough. He says it feels like a ton of bricks are on his chest."

"My goodness, Jude that sounds like a heart attack to me. You call 911 and see what they tell you to do. This blizzard is just too strong for me to venture over there. I'll check with your dad as soon as he gets in from chores. Call me back when you get a chance. Remember to say a quick prayer!"

I checked on him again and he didn't seem any better, so I called 911.

"911, What is your emergency?" the operator answered before the second ring.

"My friend, I think he is having a heart attack!"

"His name and address, please."

I gave the lady his address while I kept my eye on Mr. Olson.

"How old is Quin Olson?"

"Sixty-four."

"Is the patient conscious?"

"Yes."

"I'm checking on road conditions."

"He says his chest is very tight."

"Okay, this storm is really bad, so can you meet the ambulance at Highway 71."

Boy did that ever catch me off guard. "I guess so."

"Here's my direct number." She rattled off a phone number to me. "Call me when you have an estimated time that you will be at Highway 71."

"Okay. Let me double check this number."

I hung up after checking the number she gave me. My phone started ringing soon after hanging up.

"Hello, Jude. How is he doing?" Mom asked.

"Not good. We need to get him to Highway 71 and load him up on the ambulance."

"That's two miles away, Jude! How do you propose to get that done in this blizzard?"

"Let me talk with Dad. Maybe we could use Pete and Joe." As I waited for Dad, I checked the temperature outside. It was now zero.

"Son, what do you need?" Dad asked.

"We need to get Mr. Olson to the highway to meet the ambulance. Do you think you can hitch Pete and Joe and come get us?"

There was a long hesitation. "Oh, I don't like it, but it is probably our only chance. The storm is supposed to get worse before it gets better. I'll hitch and head that way, while you get Mr. Olson ready."

"Sure enough."

I called the dispatcher and told them our plans. I checked Mr. Olson. He seemed even more pale as he held his chest.

"Jude, I'm sorry to put you through—"

"I don't want to hear it. Now we got things to do. What stuff do you want to take with you?"

"I was always told ya can't take it with you."

I stopped what I was doing and looked him in the eye. "No, sir, Mr. Olson, you ain't going to heaven on my watch. You're going to be just fine."

"Jude, I'm not so sure. I've never felt so tough before, yet so at peace with God."

"Now listen here, you promised to be at my wedding and I've always taken you at your word. So let's pray and give this to God."

I knelt by his bed asking God for His mercy and grace. For a moment the time stood still and it even seemed like the storm let up. I teared up big time and couldn't even talk. We sat there in God's silence as He filled the room with His glory. I had a feeling of power come over me like never before. Yes, things would be okay.

Mr. Olson seemed a little better after that. We got his things ready and bundled him up for the two-mile blizzard ride.

As I stood looking out the window for Dad, I said, "You sure find strange ways to get a free ride behind Pete and Joe."

I started catching glimpses of the geldings plowing their way up the drive and you could tell each step was a struggle. One last look at the thermometer told me it was now five below zero. We met Dad and Mom at the door and got Mr. Olson loaded and bundled in. I gave Pete and Joe a quick hug and off we went. I do believe God was still with us because the storm didn't seem quite as bad as before. We could see the electric poles every once in awhile as we headed east. The geldings held their heads low as they plowed through the knee-deep snow. The drifts were three or four feet in places.

It seemed like a long time before we could see the lights on the ambulance. Pete and Joe didn't know what to think as the paramedics waded towards us with a stretcher. Joe snorted at them the closer they got. We loaded Mom and Mr. Olson up as fast as we could and Dad and I turned for home.

I don't think we went two hundred yards before all hell broke loose. The storm intensified as we drove straight into its bowels. I couldn't see anything as I drove and we soon came to a stop. I kissed to them to go and they balked and fussed the more I asked.

Dad yelled over the roaring wind, "Can you see what's ahead, Jude?"

"No!"

"Ya better get down and check it out!"

I wrapped the lines up with my frozen hands and jumped into the thigh-deep snow to see what was the hold up. I carefully followed Joe's flank until I got in front of them.

As I grabbed each rope halter I said, "Come on Pete, Joe, what's the matter?"

I pulled a little and they didn't budge. When I took a few steps back I learned why. We were heading toward the steep ditch embankment. I had driven them right towards the ditch because I couldn't see.

"Thanks Pete, thanks Joe. Sorry!"

I told Dad what happened when I got back on the rack. "Son, I think it best if you just give them their mouths and tell them to get us home! They know the way better than we do."

"Okay." I turned them straight. "Pete, Joe, get us home, boys! Get us home!"

Dad and I said a quick prayer as the geldings trudged through the thigh-deep snow. It seemed like we were going the right direction, but we couldn't tell for sure. The electric poles were out of sight from the blinding snow. All we could do was trust God and the geldings. I guess there was a ditch on each side of us, so they could sense that as they plodded along. Dad and I sat there for what seemed like hours.

Our hands were getting colder by the minute and we couldn't take it any longer. I stopped the horses and we crammed our frozen hands up into the lower part of Joe's and Pete's butt cheeks. As I stood there, I could feel my own cheeks getting stiffer. My face was starting to get frostbite. I soon had my face planted between Joe's butt cheeks also. Oh my, it felt good to get feeling back into my hands and cheeks. Yes, you guessed it! As I stood there with my face planted in Joe's cheeks, he decided to pass some gas. Wow, that was enough to part my hair and make my eyes water!

I crawled back on the rack and off we went, Pete and Joe choosing their own way home. Dad and I sat there with our backs to the wind, actually looking east as the geldings headed west. They seemed to turn right at one point, which I hoped was our driveway. It was amazing that Dad and I couldn't see anything that whole time, but next thing we knew the geldings had stopped and we were at the west end of the barn. Dad and I hustled to unhook them from the bobsled and get them in the barn. I noticed the thermometer on the outside of the barn read twenty below zero. We closed the door behind them and turned on the lights. That's when we noticed how tough Pete and Joe looked! They were completely iced over from sweat. Their nostrils were half frozen shut with a little blood coming out, and their eyes were almost froze shut. Their muscles were going into spasms and their breathing was very loud. I stood there in disbelief. What had I done to them? I couldn't help but cry as I held each one in my arms.

I blubbered out, "Pete, Joe, thank you." As my eyes flooded with more tears I prayed, "God, please help Pete and Joe, and Mr. Olson."

I cupped my hands over their noses to help them fight the

frost. It was super cold but I didn't care. I unharnessed them as Dad called Becky and told her we were home. As Pete and Joe stood in the barn aisle, I loved and loved on them for what they did. They were so tired from fighting the deep snow that their muscles were still twitching. I rubbed and rubbed their muscles till they quit twitching. I piled fresh straw in their stalls before leading them in. I would wait till chore time to feed them so they wouldn't get sick.

Dad and I waded through the snow to get in the house where we could look at his frostbite. Becky had hot cocoa waiting for us and was checking the internet for treatment for frostbite. All in all, it was a very successful trip. Praise God that we were safe.

Now that I knew Dad would be okay, I kept asking myself, were Pete and Joe going to be alright?

Chapter 7
"Horse Logging and Frame Cutting"

Mom called to tell us the ambulance made it to the hospital with Mr. Olson. They were testing him for several things but were pretty sure he had some artery blockage. The doctors told Mom he should be okay if they could do surgery in the morning to open up some arteries near his heart.

Becky tended to Dad's frostbite while I headed back to the barn with an armful of old towels to rub the geldings down and help them dry out. They were both laying down in the stalls when I got there, and they didn't seem in a big hurry to get up. I laid a bunch of towels across Pete as I rubbed on Joe. They both laid there motionless with their eyes barely open. The dairy barn was pretty warm compared to outside temps, so I think they were just absorbing as much heat as they could. The steam rolled off them as they laid there, their breathing just about normal. After chores, Dad and I got them up so they wouldn't get so stiff. They each groaned as they lifted their 2,100 pounds off the stall floor. We led them up and down the barn aisle a couple times and massaged their leg muscles. Dad and I both agreed they would be alright.

The storm lasted a total of three days with about nineteen inches of snow and lots of drifting. Right after the storm was done the temperature dropped like a rock. Most mornings we would wake to thirty or thirty-five below zero. Between chores, moving snow, and keeping water thawed, Dad and I were pretty busy. I snowshoed over to Mr. Olson's to do his chores and help Dad move snow at both places. There were a couple of places where the snow drifts were seven feet tall. Luckily, we never lost power during the storm.

The roads were finally cleared enough for Dad to run down and retrieve Mom from the hospital. The surgery had gone well and Mr. Olson was able to come home sooner than expected. He gradually worked his way back into chores and fully recovered. It was good to see him back to his old self.

My trimming business was going better than I had expected and the money was starting to build up. I started to think of finding my own place to live. I checked with a few realtors in the area to see if anything was available that would be big enough for me and the geldings. Dad, Mom and I were looking at a place near Paynesville, Minnesota. It was a couple miles west of town and came with twenty acres, a small barn, and an old farm house. The house was in need of a match, but the barn was in very good shape. The barn could store hay and some equipment, and there was pasture and a small field to maybe grow some hay. I was pretty excited about the whole opportunity. I stood there dreaming of where the new home would stand and thinking about Judy being a big part of my life. On the way home, we made a list of the positives and negatives. We crunched numbers related to down payments, monthly payments, upkeep, insurance, and building a new home. I met with the banker and soon I signed the dotted line for my own place.

First we tore down the house and saved some of the lumber. I was able to get a used house trailer for a song and that became my new temporary home. Next it was fencing time and Mr. Olson even came over to help with that.

"Why certainly, why certainly, this will be a fine place for you and Judy to raise some kids," he laughed.

"What did you say? I'm not even married yet and you're thinking about little rug rats taking over this place."

He sat down on the tailgate of the truck with that look in his eye. "Are you going to have the wedding here or at your pa's place?"

"That's up to the highfalutin' wedding planner we hire. He lives just east of Dad and has one of the finest teams of Percherons this side of the Mississippi."

"Why certainly, why certainly."

"Well, Mr. Wedding Planner, what do you see happening at

this wedding of mine? And how do you know you're even going to be invited?"

"Let me think." He scratched his chin. "You're only going to do this once, so it has to be just so. I think ya better ask your mother and Judy what they want. But I do know of a guy that could drive that fine team of hitch geldings if he was invited to that glorious day."

Harold, Perry, and Wade helped me move onto the big ranch one cold November day. They also helped get the skirting on the trailer and all buttoned up for winter. That first night sleeping in my own home was pretty special, even with the wind blowing like crazy outside. Yes, I was a bachelor waiting for Judy to get done with school. I have to admit I missed Ma's cooking big time. Cooking food is one gift the good Lord did not bestow on me.

Judy was in her last year of nursing school and looking forward to being done. We talked almost daily by phone and she came home some weekends. The more time I spent with Judy, the more I fell in love with her. Everything about her was beautiful: her love of God, her hair, her smile, her work ethic. She got along with my family and loved little kids, too. I found myself thinking of her often as I drove between hoof trimming jobs.

I started attending a Baptist church in Paynesville and was able to form a youth group with the high school kids. God had blessed me. I had my own place, my family, the geldings, and I hoped to get married after I built our new home. I wasn't about to ask my new bride to live in that tin can of a trailer. I stopped at a few lumber yards and looked at house plans, but nothing really caught my eye.

I was trimming horses at Jim Stein's, a new client of mine, and fell in love with their barn. Jim said it was timber frame construction, wooden pegs and all. He gave me the grand tour and I asked many questions.

"Jude, I heard you bought the old Zimner place." Jim said as we finished the tour of his barn.

"Yes, I did."

"That house looked very tough from the road. Are you fixing it up?"

"Nope, we fixed that with a demo crew. There's nothing left but the basement hole. I moved a house trailer in until I build a new home."

Jim rubbed his hands together to keep them warm. "Let's go

inside where it is warmer and I have an idea I think you'll like."

We sat at his kitchen table and had some hot cocoa and chocolate chip cookies as Jim started in on his idea. "So you liked the pegged barn. Have you ever thought of building a timber frame home?"

Not sure if that ever happened to you, but the moment he said that, I was sold on the idea. I dropped my cookie in the hot cocoa and instantly started dreaming of the possibilities. God soon brought me back to reality when money came to my mind.

"Jim, that is a great idea, but I assume the cost would be out of sight." I shook my head as I was still hooked on his idea. "You know, I've been to several lumber yards and looked at house plans but found nothing I liked."

"Jude, come over here." Jim walked us to his dining room window. "What do you see out there?"

I stood there awhile, dumbfounded. "I see a small field and a woods is all."

We sat back down at his kitchen table. "Do you still own those big work horses?"

"Yes."

"Mrs. and I have been wanting to clear some of those trees out. Now if I was twenty years younger and owned a nice pair of work horses and wanted to build a timber frame home, then I would be hitching that team and doing some logging with those boys to see what they're made of!"

He got up and filled our cocoa cups again. "Jude, you're a fine Christian man and the Lord has blessed me financially. So here is the offer, you can log that woods out for the beams you need to build yourself a timber frame home. The payment we need for that privilege is a free sleigh ride every winter for life and an invite to the frame raising."

I dropped a second cookie in the old hot cocoa. I was speechless, my mind a whirlwind of thoughts. In my mind I already had Pete and Joe pulling out big logs. This was unbelievable!

"Jim, I don't know what to say!" I stood up. "That offer is pretty hard to say no to! I'm not sure if I know how to build a timber frame." I gazed out the widow looking at the woods.

"That's what they sell books for, Jude." He laughed. "Now you let me know by next week what you decide."

"Thank you, Jim. I will study on this and let you know, soon.

Can I take one more peek at your barn before I leave?"

"Sure, help yourself."

Wow! My mind was doing double time as I slowly walked through his barn, this time with a whole new agenda. I stood there and studied all the joints where vertical posts tied in with horizontal beams held together with wooden pegs. I even caught myself imagining how the home would lay out with a loft and all the rooms. I left his drive totally focused on making this happen. I got home that night and scoured the internet for "timber frame" information and ordered two books on how to cut your own frame. Waiting for those books was easier said than done. They both arrived the same day and I stayed up till two AM reading them. Yes I had the bug and it didn't seem to be going away. I soon gave Jim a "yes" for an answer and measured his barn over and over. Jim and I walked his woods and he marked trees we could take. I asked Jim if I could bring Dad, Mom and Judy out to look.

Devotions that night really hit home as it was on Ecclesiastes 3:3: "A time to tear down and a time to build," and Psalm 127:1 "Unless the Lord builds the house, its builders labor in vain." God was behind this whole deal, first lining up the land, tearing down the old house and finding Jim, who tells me what I should consider for a home. The main problem I saw was in my haste to get going I had not thanked God and sought his council.

"Lord in Heaven, forgive me for my sins. I have been too busy to include you on this whole deal, especially when you're the one that set it all up in the first place! Who am I to deserve all that you give, Lord? Lord, I thank you and ask your blessing of safety and courage as I build this home with your grace."

I decided to keep the secret of the style of home from Judy till we had the frame raising. But to test her, I took her over to Jim's place one weekend and walked her through his barn to see what she thought of it. I told her I needed to check on a horse. As I pretended to check on Jim's horse, Judy stood and gazed at his barn. This was looking good.

"Jude, have you ever seen a barn like this before?"

"Oh, I guess I didn't give it much thought. Do you like it?"

She reached out and touched a beam. "It's beautiful! Look at the size of the beams and how massive they look. I wonder how old this is?"

"You could ask Jim if you want to know. I usually trim outside so I've barely been in the barn before." I walked out trying to stop from laughing and pretending I didn't care about the barn and its massive beams. God had given me my answer.

Dad and I spent two solid days measuring and cutting trees in Jim's woods. We were able to cut mostly dead oak trees and some ash. The main thing you look for is straight trunks. One oak log we dropped was close to 38 feet long and straight as an arrow. I wondered if the geldings could even pull something that big and heavy.

That next Saturday I got up early and headed to the barn. "Pete and Joe, are you ready for a day of logging?" I asked them as I brushed and harnessed them. I will never get tired of the thundering sound of their hooves when I load them into the horse trailer. Dad and Mr. Olson met me at the woods. Mr. Olson brought an old logging skid with him and a cant hook. We had about six inches of snow on the ground, which is ideal as it helps keep the logs out of the mud.

"We'll see what them boys are made of after we hook them to that oak log," Mr. Olson laughed as he stood by the 38 footer. "Jude, I would hook to a couple smaller logs first and then hook to the big one while they're still fresh."

It was great to have Mr. Olson there. He had logged with his dad when he was a kid, so he knew what to do. I was nervous as I line drove Pete and Joe up to the first log, since they had never done this before. I picked up the evener and backed them up to a 16-foot ash log. Dad got us hooked up as Pete and Joe nervously danced back and forth.

"Jude, you have to stay off to the side so that log can't roll up on you!" Mr. Olson said.

I looked at Dad and he gave me a head nod. "Pete and Joe, get up." I commanded. They stepped forward, and soon the evener was off the ground with tug chains tight. I took a quick look back at the log and it was moving. This was easy! Next thing I knew, Pete and Joe broke into a trot with me running behind them.

"Jude, rein them in, pull them back!" Mr. Olson hollered.

"Easy boys, easy." I dug my feet in and tried to slow them down. Nope, they had other plans. Let me tell you that first log came out in record time. I was breathing hard when I finally got them stopped at the edge of the woods. I stopped and thought about that quick trip and decided that wasn't a lot of fun!

Pete and Joe were still wired as I struggled to get them

unhooked. "Whoa boys, easy!" I held them with one hand as I fought the log tongs with the other. I finally got them unhooked and headed back for a second log.

Dad and Mr. Olson were waiting by the next log. "Jude, now listen to me, no looking back this time. You stay with them geldings and don't give them any slack in the lines. You cannot trot at all or you'll end up with a wreck. Understand?" Mr. Olson seemed mad at me.

I knew I could do better, so with the lines gripped firmly in my hands we started the second log. Pete and Joe tried to break into a trot as I held on tight. They arched their necks and fought the bits, but I held them right where there should be as we walked the second log out. With 4,200 pounds of wired muscle in front of you, the power you have in your hands is hard to imagine. When I got back, I could hear Mr. Olson mumbling "why certainly." By the third log, Pete and Joe were starting to understand the program.

Number four log was the 38 foot oak beast. We had to get it up in the skidding sled, so Pete and Joe pulled it sideways a couple feet until it was on the sled. Dad chained it to the sled while I brought the geldings to the front of it.

"I'm not sure if they can even pull this log at all. They might try to balk on you, so be ready. If they can pull it, you'll have to stop and rest them every so often." Mr. Olson explained.

Dad gave me the thumbs up and I stood and looked back at the size of that log. I said a quick prayer and turned back to the geldings. "Pete and Joe, get up!" They leaned into the load and Joe soon balked as he felt the heavy weight. He gave it another try as Pete quit. We were see-sawing back and forth and going nowhere fast. "Whoa!" I pulled back on the lines.

I knew that couldn't happen again. I got them settled down, squared up, and with an extra firm command shouted. "Pete and Joe get up!" They leaned into the collars again to give it another try. I watched their heads like a hawk and sure enough, they were starting to give up again. I was on them right now. "Pete, Joe, come on! Give it to me!" I yelled at the top of my lungs. Their ears turned my way and they started gradually moving forward. I could hear the log losing its grip on the ground. Pete and Joe were getting down and scratching for all they were worth! The tugs were as tight as banjo strings as they slowly won the battle. It takes air to move that much weight and you could see the pink of their nostrils as they flared out, grabbing for all the air they could get. I gave them free rein so they had freedom to swing their heads in all directions. With each choppy step the massive log was moving south as the geldings gave it their all. They pulled it about thirty yards and I stopped them for a well deserved rest. I laid the lines down and went up and rubbed their necks. "Good boys, good boys! You made me proud."

Mr. Olson stood to the side and smiled. "Jude, I have to admit, I never thought they would touch that log. That pull came from their hearts! Why certainly, why certainly. There aren't very many teams in the country that could take on that load!"

"Thanks, Mr. Olson! Pete and Joe, did you hear that? We didn't win any ribbons at the fair, but we can sure pull a load."

It took four different pulls and rest stops to get that 38 footer snaked out of the woods. While they were still tired from that pull, we hitched them to several trees that had hung up in other trees. That means the gelding had to finish pulling a tree down, so basically it ended up crashing to the ground while they pulled. They trotted out a little as the first couple trees came down behind them, but were too tired to fight the lines much. The rest of the day was uneventful and we were even able to run a chainsaw a couple feet from Pete and Joe without spooking them at all. By the end of the day, we had maybe half the logs pulled out and two very tired geldings. I pulled the harnesses off the geldings and threw their winter blankets on them. "You guys did me proud today. What would I do without you?" I rubbed the base of their ears.

We ended up pulling logs two other days to get the rest of the logs pulled out. Dad and I hauled them over to Grady's mill and gave him our list of what we needed. I spent the next few weeks of spare time going over my drawings with a fine tooth comb. I had to buy some chisels, mortise bits, cant hook, and a heavy duty 12 inch circular saw. I had to make two heavy saw horses, and I welded up a steel tire little beam cart that would allow me to move beams around by myself. As soon as Grady was done, I was now ready to start cutting the frame.

Each night I would lay in bed thinking through each process of cutting the frame to the frame raising. This was the best time for me to double check that I had everything ready. I also dreamed of a finished timber frame home and what it might be for Judy and me.

Two weeks later Grady called and the beams were ready. Now the thinking work would begin. Dad and I hauled the beams home and got them stickered and under a tarp. My life was busy between trimming horses, leading youth, cutting a frame, and spending time with Judy on the phone. My goal was to have a frame cut for a frame raising by early fall. That would give me most of spring and summer to get it complete.

I'll never forget that first time cutting beams: I stood there and stared at the stack of 8 by 8 beams thinking I was kidding myself. I finally talked myself into pulling the first beam onto my homemade saw horses. I measured and re-measured that beam about ten times. I marked off the tenon and the knee mortises with a lumber pencil and square. I grabbed my brand new 12 inch circular saw and made my first cut with hands shaking a little. I stopped and checked it several times and made the second cut. I soon had my first tenon completed on a 10 foot vertical 8 by 8 post. I put the 2 inch mortise bit into the drill and started on the first knee mortise. The drill struggled as the bit crawled into the oak beam. The oaks chips bubbled out above the bit as it cut a perfect 2 inch hole. I drilled two holes for the mortise on the other side of the beam and was ready for the chisels: first the 2 inch flat chisel and mallet and then a corner chisel and mallet. It took me some time to figure out how to stop the chisels from cutting at a wrong angle. I went back and forth from the flat to corner chisel and soon had one mortise done. I flipped the log over and started on the second mortise. I was feeling pretty good on my progress until I swung the mallet and hit my thumb. Ouch! That was going to leave a mark. I held my thumb and I stood back and looked at my two mortises. They looked a little rough, but for my first ever they were acceptable. This was going better than I thought. I cut a test knee out and made sure it fit in the mortises. With my confidence soaring, I marked my first beam with my code, took a few pictures, and set it off to the side. I only had around 156 more mortises to go and about the same in tenons to do.

That summer was crazy busy. I only slept about five hours each night. I was up by four AM with quartz lights cutting and drilling beams. Then off to trim feet on horses till around six PM and back home for more beam work till 9:30 to 10:00PM. Many times when Judy would call me I was in the middle of beams, posts, and tools.

When talking with Judy, my biggest challenge was not

mentioning the frame cutting. "How is the prettiest nurse at Crown College doing?"

"Oh Jude, I miss you, but I'm doing fine. How are you doing?"

"Fine, but I really miss you and I find myself thinking about you all the time. I can't wait for you to graduate." I wanted to tell her everything about the frame so I changed the subject. "The good news is I'm getting new clients for trimming, so that is encouraging. And can you believe I'm up to 24 mice caught in the trailer. When I go to bed I can hear them running through the walls and ceiling."

"Yuck! How can you stand that? They are so creepy." She sighed. "You know, I miss Pete and Joe, too. How are they doing?"

"They're fine, fat as ever. When you graduate we're going to load up a picnic basket and head to Sibley State Park for a nice long trail ride."

"That sounds like fun, I can't wait! Speaking of graduation, I might stay for summer school and prepare for state boards in August. I need all the help I can get for the state board exam. Enough about school, have you done any more thinking on a new home?"

I had to bite my lip as I spoke. "Not really. It seems so expensive. Maybe I'll just buy a newer trailer house."

There was a hesitation at her end. "Oh, well, I guess I never thought of that. So what are you doing with all your spare time?"

"I've been reading and exercising more, helping Dad with a few projects."

Judy and I prayed with and for each other and said our goodbyes. How many times have I heard the phrase ''absence makes the heart grow fonder?'' Well, after each phone call I truly believed it. With Judy staying in school for the summer, that gave me more time to work on cutting the frame.

I spent the rest of the summer cutting the frame in the early mornings and evenings. It was more of a project than I thought, measuring and re-measuring to make sure everything would fit. I had to take the geldings back to the woods again and snake a few more logs. I finally finished all the main posts and beams, then I started on all the knees. I thought I would never finish cutting knees. They were just plain boring to cut. I rewarded myself after cutting all those knees with making some wooden mallets. I made two big boys for forcing the tenons into the mortises and three small ones for pounding pegs. They were a blast to make. Checking the calendar with Judy and Mom, I decided to raise the frame on Labor Day weekend. Dad, Gramps, and Mr. Olson came over a couple weeks before the big day to put one bent together.

Mr. Olson stood by my collection of wooden mallets and picked each one up for an inspection. "Why certainly."

A bent for this frame was four posts with knees and a tie beam. This frame had five bents total and I would save the other bents for the frame raising. I just needed to put one bent together for my own piece of mind. I had to laugh at Mr. Olson. I think he ended up pounding in every peg on that bent. We each took turns with the big mallets, swinging away convincing the tenons to go into the mortises. We had to pull several apart to trim tenons down or work the chisels more. That took more time than what I wanted. Four hours later we had bent number one complete.

We all stood back and admired our handy work as Gramps said, "Jude, I have to admit, you've done a fine job. This must have taken you hours of cutting and chiseling, wow! But you need to pre-fit every one of those joints before the frame raising or you'll spend all day fighting them."

"Yeah, I hate to say you're right, but look at how much time it took today." I complained.

"How about if I come over and help you the next couple days?" Gramps asked.

"You talked me into it!"

They all left and I checked on the geldings and had a little supper. After supper I went back out and sat on the tie beam of the bent we put together and just admired the structure. I would follow a post up to where it met the girt, knee, and tie beam, and then follow the tie beam over to the next post. I sat there for more than an hour praising God for allowing me the courage to tackle such a project. From the trees that He created, to the horses He created, to the skills He gave me and the perseverance He gave me through His written word, God is good!

I talked Becky into helping me with the invitations, so she came over to look at the frame. We took some pictures of the mallets and the completed bent for the invite we would send out. We made a special one for Judy; hers mentioned a barn raising. I wanted her to think this was for another barn instead of a home.

"Becky, I'm thinking of asking Judy to marry me during

this frame raising somehow. Do you see any reason Judy and I shouldn't get married?"

She got a big smile on her face and threw her arms around my neck, giving me a huge hug. "Jude, I knew the day you brought her in the house after her little wreck that you and her would get married someday!"

"Are you kidding me?"

"Nope! I wonder if during the frame raising is a good time with everyone busy and stuff, unless you did it at the very end or the next day? You know, God has worked a miracle in Judy, and you two compliment each other very well."

"Thanks, little sis! I'll have to think about when it is best and also ask permission from Mr. Clemons. I'm also going to check with Mom and Dad."

We sent the invites out and a couple days later, as Gramps and I were fine tuning the frame, several people stopped to see what this was all about. My neighbor stopped and couldn't believe what he was looking at. He had a wedding to attend, so he said he couldn't make it. He just stood there staring at the oak and ash beams.

Late that night the phone rang. "Hello?"

"You creep, why didn't you tell me about this barn you've been building?" Judy laughed.

"Creep? You must have the wrong number! The guy that lives here is no creep. He might stretch the truth at times or not tell you the whole story, but he is the guy in love with a princess who is going to pass her state nursing boards."

"I miss you soo much, Jude! When I got your invitation for the barn raising, I sat down and cried."

"I'm sorry, why would you do that?"

"I been so stressed out and missing home and missing you, it caught me off guard and I just crumbled."

"If I was there, we would have gone for a nice long walk in the moonlight and I would have held your hand and sang to you."

"Oh, Jude, do you want me to start crying again?"

"Someday, I'll hold you and you can cry on my shoulder all you want. Remember on your parents' swing when you sat on my lap and cried?"

I heard a few sniffles through the phone. "You creep, I just want to be near you and you get all mushy!"

"I love to hear this type of cry over the phone, Judy.

Remember in James it talks of perseverance, and you only have about three more weeks and you're done." There was a long pause as I could hear Judy wiping tears. "I invited your parents to the barn raising. I wonder if they'll come?"

"Not sure. Well, I'm going to study for boards some more and get to bed. Please pray for me. Good night, love you."

"Miss you! Love you!"

After hanging up, I sat in my easy chair thinking of how to pop the question to Judy. I also wondered how to ask Mr. Clemons for his daughter's hand. I started dreaming of how Judy would react to our wood beams being for her home and about the marriage proposal. The joy I had in my heart was so special, I was in love and very blessed. I read some in my Bible and went to bed.

The next day I was trimming horses near Judy's home place, so I drove in hoping to catch Mr. Clemons at home. I looked across the yard and there stood the cottonwood tree with the board swing blowing in the wind. Mr. Clemons was in the garage fixing his lawnmower.

I reluctantly approached him. "Hi, Mr. Clemons, how you doing?"

"Oh, I'm fine I guess, but this lawnmower has decided to skip the middle section every pass I make."

"It's probably a loose blade or a belt," I said.

"That mechanical stuff is for the birds. I'm not sure what to do." He sat down on an old milk crate and wiped his brow.

"Let me take a look at it for you, Mr. Clemons." I pulled all the extra grass clippings off the top of the deck and checked the belts. They seemed okay.

"Do you have a trouble light?" I asked.

"Sure, hanging on the south wall above the air compressor."

I plugged the trouble light in and looked under the deck. Sure enough, the middle blade was very loose. I had to jack the front end up to get to the nut to tighten it with a big crescent wrench. The whole time fixing, I was working up the courage to ask for Judy's hand in marriage. I lowered the mower back down and sat on the floor looking at Mr. Clemons.

"It should work fine now, Mr. Clemons." I got up and started pacing the floor.

"Really? That didn't take you very long."

"Mr. Clemons, I need to ask you something that's very important to me." He looked away from me and scratched the side of his face. I was nervous as a lobster at a seafood party. "I've been courting Judy now for about three years and I'm in love and I want to marry you."

What! Did I just say what I thought I said? I think I told Mr. Clemons that I wanted to marry him! I turned red as a beet and started stammering for new words. How could I be that stupid? I looked at him and he was shaking his head back and forth.

"Young man, I think you need to think real hard about what you just said." He laughed a little while and he looked my way. "Now settle down and think real hard about which Clemons you want to marry!"

"I'm sorry Mr. Clemons, I've never done this before!" I swayed back and forth like I had ants in my pants. "What I meant to say is, I love Judy and would like to ask your permission for her hand in marriage." I let out a big sigh of relief and wiped the sweat from my brow.

He stood up and looked out toward the cottonwood tree. "Tell me why I should."

I wasn't quite ready for that question. I thought for a bit. "Well, first of all, Judy is a very special girl and I want to protect her, cherish her, provide for her, and love her for the rest of our lives. Second, I love her more than anything else in the world except for God. And third, Judy loves me."

"Jude, why would you come to an old drunk and ask for Judy's hand?" His eyes welled up with tears as he reached for his hankie in his back pocket.

"You're her father, who else would I ask?"

"You've changed my daughter for the better in many ways, Jude. I'm not sure if I even know her anymore. Maybe I never did know her. I was too busy chasing a bottle." He turned my way and looked me right in the eyes. "Promise me you'll take care of her and never drink your life away?"

"I promise, sir."

"You have my permission, or my blessing, whatever I'm supposed to say."

"Mr. Clemons, thank you so much. I will take good care of her and I want you to know Judy loves you."

His eyes filled with tears as I turned and walked away. I crawled in my pick-up, took one last look at the swing, and slowly backed out of the driveway. I was one step closer to being engaged, and I was never so happy. I stopped by Mom's and

Dad's and helped Dad with milking. Mom came out and talked while Dad and I milked.

"Mom, Dad, I'm thinking of asking Judy to marry me the weekend of the frame raising. Do you see any problems with that?" I asked as I put the milker on number 28.

Mom turned her head and smiled. "We were wondering when you were going to get around to it. Dad and I assumed you would be asking when she finished school. As far as I know, you have both our blessings."

Dad started laughing. "Just as long as Judy doesn't make the wedding cake, I'll be there, God willing." Dad came over and took the milker off number 28 for me. I was in a daze. "I guess that will put more pressure on you to get that frame finished. Pretty soon I'll be sleeping with Grandma." He laughed as he leaned over a cow, looking at Mom.

"Bud Bonner, they aren't even married and you're thinking of grandkids! Shame on you."

"Dad, do you have any reasons why I shouldn't ask Judy to marry me?"

"No son, I don't. God has transformed her into a real lady. It was special to see her grow in Christ. Now, if you don't ask her, yes sir, that would be a mistake."

"Where did you buy her ring?" Mom asked.

That hit me like number 28 kicking me. With cutting the frame and everything else, that ring thing hadn't crossed my mind.

"Might I suggest you ask your sister to go with you real soon and get that chore done?" Mom said as she smiled at me. "Men!" She shook her head.

Becky was gracious enough to go with me and help pick out a ring as it rained cats and dogs. There was a whole lot more to this than what I thought: sizing, engagement ring, wedding band and, of course, money. Becky was a huge help, along with the jeweler, and I left the store with what I came in for.

"Becky, thanks for coming. I would have hated to do that by myself. I need to ask one more favor. Can you and Mom make a blueberry pie for the frame raising and have this ring in one of the pieces, and make sure Judy gets that piece?"

"I like it, great idea. Consider it a done deal."

Chapter 8

"Frame Raising and Wedding Proposal"

I was soon staring at the day before the frame raising and had one thousand things to do before I was ready. I was in a tizzy with all that needed to be done, when I heard a truck coming up the driveway. It was Gramps. Man, was I glad to see him!

He stepped out of his pickup as he put on his gloves. "Put me to work."

I gave him about five things to do while I did others. We had to get ladders out, make gin poles, cut some wooden stakes, put pegs in 5-gallon pails, get ropes out, sort boards, and go to town to rent some scaffolding.

Before I went to town, I asked Gramps for a special request. "Gramps, I want to have an old fashioned barn ladder coming off bent number two. I have all the material on the saw horse here. It would be very special to me if you would make that for me."

He stared at the material. "Well, I don't know? How long, how wide? I have nothing to go on."

I handed him a slip of paper with all the dimensions he needed and jumped in my truck to get the scaffolding. My mind was going in many directions as I drove, mainly planning my proposal to Judy. It was fun thinking of all the ways she might react. I also assumed she would say yes. I got back from town and Gramps was doing well with the ladder, so I unloaded the scaffolding and set a few sections up. By the time I took a few more measurements to double check things, Gramps was finishing up on the ladder.

He walked my way as I stood by the frame. "Are you ready for your big day tomorrow?"

"I believe I have everything checked off my list. Wow, I didn't think I would ever be able to say that."

"Do you think you're forgetting one very important item?" I gave him a puzzled look. "Have you prayed over this site and frame and asked for safety and God's blessings?"

I felt foolish to a certain degree, because I hadn't. "No, sir, I haven't. Will you pray with me right now?"

Gramps and I knelt right there with our arms on the first bent and asked the Lord for His protection. Gramps asked Him to bless this as a home for my future spouse and I. I thanked Jesus for all he had given me: my health, my family, Pete and Joe, this place, and Judy. I thanked Gramps and he headed home while I went in to get cleaned up.

It was sleepless in rural Paynesville that night for me. I bet I put that frame up twenty times as I lay there. I pictured who would do what and guessed how far we would before lunch, and what would Judy do with her piece of blueberry pie. I rolled out of bed at five AM with things to do. I did chores, checked the weather forecast, pulled all the tarps off the beams, and did my devotions before breakfast. I was reaching for my cereal bowl when I heard someone pull up the driveway. I broke out into a huge smile, as it was Judy heading my way with a grocery sack in her arms.

I ran out to meet her and gave her a big hug. "You got up awful early this morning! It is so good to see you."

"Oh Jude, I couldn't sleep and I couldn't wait any longer, so I figured I might as well cook you a big breakfast." She looked me in the eyes. "Do you know I'm in love?"

We started to walk toward the house trailer. "So you're in love, and who might you be in love with?"

She stopped and handed me the grocery sack. "Well, he's a godly man, he's about your size, he's strong yet kind, he owns two big horses, and someday I hope to marry him!"

I blew out a big breath of air when she mentioned the word "marry." She gave me a funny look. I could hardly hold myself back from telling her the whole plan.

"So, what's for breakfast, ma'am?"

She smiled as she started to unload the sack of groceries. "I figured you should eat flapjacks, sausage links, extra thick bacon, hot cinnamon rolls and some OJ." I sat there as she dug through my kitchen looking for a skillet or something. I poured a small glass of OJ and was taking a sip when she asked, "So, where is this timber frame barn going?"

That was it! I lost it. I blew that OJ all over the kitchen. She stopped and looked at me. "Jude Bonner, what's going on? What did I say that made you blow up?" I sat there and wiped my smile off with my sleeve as I fought to keep my composure.

She shook her finger at me. "You're up to something, now what is it? Maybe I should just eat this fancy breakfast by myself."

"When you said 'barn' I instantly thought of something that needed doing before we can start, that's all." I got up and looked out the window so she couldn't see my expression. I soon had two arms wrapped around me from the back.

With her head on my back shoulder she squeezed me hard. "Jude Bonner, I'm not so sure if I believe a word you say! I'm going to be watching you very close today, honey."

Judy's breakfast was not quite as good as I hoped. I'm not sure how a person can mess up pancakes, but they tasted like they had sawdust and wood glue in them. It took several glasses of OJ to get then down the old windpipe. But I lied again and told her it was wonderful. I helped her clean up the kitchen a little and we both headed outside just as Mom and Dad pulled in. Mr. Olson was right behind them with Becky.

Mom and Becky gave Judy a big hug as Mr. Olson walked our way with a broad smile on his face. "Jude, where are you putting this timber frame home at, is it the same spot the old home sat?"

Judy tilted her head down and looked my way. "Mr. Olson, did you say home?"

"Why certainly! It says that right here on my invite, look for yourself."

He handed Judy his invite. "Hmmm... you are invited to a timber frame HOME raising at the Jude Bonner ranch, Labor Day weekend?" She quietly handed his invite back and walked past me and whispered, "Barn raising, caught you already."

I sheepishly answered back. "I never lie, unless I'm alone or with someone, Judy."

The people were piling in the driveway and everyone was all excited to get started. We had old, young, men and women, all with big smiles on their faces. Gramps and I had everyone stand around the beams and he said a quick prayer.

I climbed up on the pile of 8 by 8's and gave some instructions. "Thank you for coming, we really appreciate this. I want to personally thank Jim Stein for all that he has done for this day. Now, it is important that you listen to me as I know what pieces go where, and hopefully no one should get hurt. That is bent number one laying here, so we have four more to put together. There are big wooden mallets that you can use to force the posts into the beams. The smaller mallets are for pounding pegs." We were interrupted by a car pulling into the driveway. Everyone turned to see who it was. I had to smile as Judy's parents stepped out of the van, work gloves and a pan of food. I waved to them and turned back to finish my instructions. "I need to give the okay before any pegs are driven in and no one uses a regular hammer on any part of the frame at all. Now each post has a number on the bottom, so let's break up into three teams, and each team will start on a bent. Dad, Gramps, and Mr. Olson will each be in charge of a team."

As soon as I quit talking people started moving for the post pile. It was like they were in a race, they were calling out numbers and hauling posts and beams around the foundation. It was all I could do to keep up with guiding the three groups.

Many times you'd hear, "Where is one of those big mallets?" The dull thud from the mallets echoed across the yard. It took about an hour and we had three bents put together with- out pegs. I hollered from a ladder. "You may now drive the pegs home. Please let the younger ones of the groups give it a try."

In short order each team was swinging their small mallets. It was a blessing to stand back and watch people working together. Becky took many pictures in between helping Grampa's team.

I stood back and surveyed the scene. We had four bents laying there waiting to be tipped up. It was kind of funny, everyone was waiting for the next instructions. "Now the fun begins! We need mostly men shoulder-to-shoulder along the tie beam of bent number one. Ladies and kids can handle the ropes, and someone has to be ready to scab 2 by 4s at the side of each post once we get it vertical. We also need people on the pike poles to help push it up. We will lift on my count of three." I walked over and stood in the middle of the tie beam and gave more instructions. "The ropes stop it from tipping once it is vertical, so pay attention if you're on a rope."

I looked left and right and we had close to twenty-five guys bent over ready to lift. "One, two, three!" I shouted. It was awesome! That bent creaked as it slowly went up among groans from the guys. "Not too fast guys, easy." We got it up around chest level and kind of came to a stalemate; gravity was working very well. "We need more help here!" Several people standing by ran in and gave us the extra boost to keep it going in the right direction. Ladies and kids were pulling on the ropes and we soon had bent number one standing vertical.

Wow! I just wanted to stand there and admire it, it was beautiful. I quickly thanked God and grabbed my level. We got bent number one plumbed and secured with the scabs of 2 by 4s and were now ready for bent number two.

By now our crew had the confidence they needed. We moved some scaffolding along the eve sides so we could reach the horizontal grits that tie the bents together. We were shoulder to shoulder again, and bent number two was on its way up. I jumped out and made sure the girts were going in okay. Girts are horizontal 4 by 5s that tie the bents together and give you a place to fasten the siding to. Bent number two was now vertical and I gave the okay for pegs to be driven. The enthusiasm of the workers was contagious. Everyone seemed to be having a great time.

Mom rang the dinner bell right after we got bent number three vertical. Pastor Hanson graced our meal and we all dove into a hearty meal of potato salad and all. As I went through the chow line mom made sure I took some of Mrs. Clemons green jello with apples. Becky was in charge of the pies and I caught her telling everyone to watch Judy eat her pie as she dished out pieces of homemade pies. Mom coerced Judy into sitting by me and taking a break from the chow line. I was on pins and needles as Becky reached over Judy's shoulder with a beautiful piece of blueberry pie. I scanned the crowd and noticed many eyes on Judy. Luckily, she was too busy talking with my Aunt Betty to notice.

I didn't think Judy was ever going to dig into her blueberry pie, between talking and just plain picking at her food. I looked out of the corner of my eye as she finally took her first bite. I wasn't the only one watching every move she made. It was becoming a little too obvious as everyone focused on Judy. With her second bite she looked up and noticed many eyes looking back at her.

She turned my way as she blushed. "Do I have something on my face or something, everyone seems to be staring at me?"

"I guess it's just your glowing radiance that has everyone captivated. Do you know how happy I am right now? Pretty good pie, huh?"

"Jude, something is going on here and I don't understand it."

"Matthew 7: 'Ask and it will be given to you; seek and you will find; knock and the door will be opened to you.' Now, if you don't finish that pie, we'll never get a door to open on this house."

She gave me one of her looks as she brought her fork down into her pie for the third time. Her fork came to an abrupt stop halfway into the cut. She looked my way.

"Must be a blueberry pit," I said.

"Blueberries don't have pits, Mr. Bonner." She started to dig with her fork and finger. Soon, part of the gold band was showing. She took a quick glance at me and dug all the faster. She separated the blueberries, sauce, and crust away from her ring as it lay there on her plate.

She stopped right there and didn't move a muscle for several seconds. Everyone was focused on Judy, and the place was dead quiet. Like water through a sieve, her tears started flowing down her cheeks. Judy was sobbing before I knew it. Jeepers! What did this mean? I knelt down on one knee beside her and put my hand on her knee. That only compounded her sobbing. I looked at Mom for direction with a puzzled look on my face. Mom gave me a re-assuring head nod back.

Judy was wiping her eyes with her napkin as Becky brought her a couple more napkins. I reached for Judy's hand and encouraged her to stand. She slowly got up and stood facing me.

I looked up at Judy's face and felt the presence of God as I spoke to her. "Judy, I would be so blessed to have your hand in marriage. Will you marry me?"

Before I knew it, Judy threw herself on my knee with her arms around my neck and flooded me with more tears. All our guests stood and cheered as I held her. I was soon fighting back my own tears as God's presence surrounded Judy and I.

I whispered into her ear between my own sobs. "I love you, and please spend the rest of your life with me in our timber frame home."

"Jude, yes, yes, yes!" she whispered back. "I love you so much, and I can't wait to be your wife." She leaned back and kissed me. The crowd exploded with more cheers!

"Judy, can we see if the ring fits?"

Judy and I stood up and she held out her left hand while I slipped the engagement ring onto her finger. It seemed just the right size. "Ladies and gentleman, I'd like to introduce you to my fiancé, Ms. Judy Clemons." Another round of cheers and whistles went up while Mom, Dad, Becky, and Mr. and Mrs. Clemons lined up for hugs.

"Hey everybody, we thank you for coming out today and helping, but I see a pile of beams waiting to go up. Let's get her done!"

I think the energy was twice as strong as before dinner, from the wedding proposal and everyone having full bellies. We split up into three crews again and posts and beams started going up. By 7:30 that night we had all the bents up, all pegs driven, roof decking on, and the loft decking in place on our saltbox timber frame. Gramps and Dad were putting the loft ladder in place while I grabbed Judy for placing the pine bough at the peak. It's an old tradition of nailing a pine bough at the peak of a newly raised frame. Mr. Olson set a ladder for us, and Judy and I climbed to the east gable end with pine bough in hand. I held the bough while Judy nailed it to the fascia board. The pine bough is a symbol to show that the trees are still taller than the frame that was just put up.

The crowd slowly dispersed as Judy and I thanked them over and over. I stood there wondering what really happened as I looked at the silhouette of the frame standing tall in front of Judy and I. The day seemed to go by in a blur. It was hard to grasp all that took place. I grabbed Judy's hand and led her to the middle of the frame and we sat on some saw horses.

"Where do you want the kitchen?" I asked Judy as she pushed her hair back. She stood up and walked through the open frame, studying the space. I just sat there and admired my fiancé as she continually looked down at her finger, thinking I wouldn't notice.

"Ya know, you're supposed to be telling me where the kitchen should be instead of staring at the hardware on your finger."

"Oh, honey, I'm just so happy right now! Can you imagine, I'll be Mrs. Jude Bonner! I can't wait."

I got up and took her by the hand. "Ms. Clemons, may I show

you the layout of your new home?" She nodded with a gleam in her eyes. "The kitchen would be best here, with an island countertop, the main bath over in that corner with utility room on the back side. We'll have a fireplace in that area with spare bedrooms beside it, the living room is the whole center section, and finally the master bed and bath in the loft."

"This is so neat, I'm the luckiest girl in the world!"

I put my arms around Judy and looked into her eyes. "You see that door opening over there? Yes ma'am, someday I'll be carrying you over that threshold. But you'll have a different name. God willing, you and I are going to grow old in this home."

She laid her head on my shoulder. I softly sang "Put your Head on my Shoulder" to her as we rocked back and forth. We held each other for a long time without saying a word while I gazed up at the stars. "Judy, I could hold you all night, but we better send you home."

"Yes, I suppose you're right, but this is so special. I love you, and thank you for this special day."

We prayed with each other and I walked her to her car.

Chapter 9
"Wedding Bells"

Judy and I decided to have our wedding on Labor Day weekend, one year after the frame raising. That should give me time to finish our home and Judy time to organize all the wedding plans.

I'm sure Pete and Joe thought I disowned them with all the time I spent trimming feet and working on the frame. We had a nice fall weather wise, so I was able to get the frame closed in with walls and a roof before winter hit. Judy also passed her state boards, so she was officially a registered nurse. To celebrate, I took a weekend off from the frame and spent it with Judy and the geldings trail riding. Pete and Joe were troopers. We must have ridden twenty miles that weekend.

Any spare time I had was spent on our home. Gramps would come over on Saturdays and help along with Dad. Judy, Becky and Mom would help when they could. We built interior walls, ran electric wires, trimmed windows, hung sheetrock, taped sheetrock, installed bath fixtures, hung wall paper, painted, and laid flooring. By early November I had hooked up our floor heating to the boiler so we were able to heat the place all winter, which turned out to be a good thing.

That winter was brutal. Many days started out below zero with the wind howling. I was fighting frozen water lines in my trailer and the barn most of the winter. The days get very long when you fight frozen pipes morning and night. The first thing I would do in the morning was check my water in the bathroom to see if it was running. If not, I would crawl under the trailer and add more heat tape or run a kerosene heater.

Pete and Joe took extra hay with the twenty below temps. The colder it gets the more energy they need to stay warm. Between frozen pipes, trimming feet, and building our home, I was plenty sick of winter. I have to admit, there were times when God and I talked about the weather.

By mid April winter finally let go and our last snow banks turned into slough water. I was ready to do cartwheels down the driveway, I was so waiting for spring! My attitude perked right up and I was a new man with the weather change. Our home was coming along better than I expected, so I took on more hoof trimming clients. I was saving for kitchen cabinets and the extra income would go toward that. Judy had her eye on custom cabinets by Malt Design Cabinets out of Belgrade. They had been doing cabinets for 30 years in the area and were known for top quality work. Judy and I met with Steve one evening and the kitchen was planned right on the spot with a tape measure and computer. By August, our custom cabinets were installed, and wow, did they ever add a finishing touch to the home!

Technically, I could have moved into our home, but I thought it best if I waited till we were married and Judy and I could spend our first night in our home together. At least I wasn't fighting frozen pipes anymore, so a few more weeks in the trailer was manageable, mice and all. I was able to sell the trailer to someone to use as a hunting shack with the agreement that they would haul it out the third week in August. I was so happy to see it heading down the driveway, never to be seen or lived in by Jude Bonner again!

Judy wanted her wedding reception at Mom's and Dad's place. With me being temporarily homeless, Pete, Joe, and I moved back home to help out. Mom had a list a mile long, so Dad needed plenty of help to get everything done. Pete and Joe got plenty of attention from Becky as she missed having them at home. With God's grace, everything was lining up for the big day like we hoped. God even blessed us with great weather.

Dad woke me early the day of the wedding. It was a gorgeous morning. We did chores early and started in on the geldings.

As Dad curried on Joe he said, "Son, your Mom and I are awful proud of you and I want you to know that your mom and I think you are doing the right thing today. Judy is a fine gal and you two will do just fine. The one thing I want you to do is to etch in your mind the first time you see Judy walking up that aisle. I would encourage you to keep that image in your head for the rest of your life, so when your eyes might wander to other women, you can bring Judy to your mind. And remember, you will be saying a vow in front of Jesus Christ today. May God bless this day."

"Yes, sir. Yes, sir."

Wade Estep stayed at our place and he and Becky came out to help. It was the full makeover for Pete and Joe with a complete bath, currying, trimmed manes and tails and ear hair, and painted hooves. Becky was going to braid manes and tails later. Pete and Joe stood tall. Harold and Perry helped Mr. Olson with the hitch wagon and the patent leather harness.

Mom was at the church helping Judy and the bridesmaids get ready. Mom's sisters were at home working like crazy on lunch and final details on the decorations in the tent. Dave Grimm, a good friend of Dad's, was there bright and early with his portable hog roaster. Everything seemed to be going as planned.

Soon I headed to church with my groomsmen: Harold, Perry, and Wade. We had some prayer time with Pastor Hanson and Carl Toney. We took some pictures before the ceremony, but I wasn't allowed to see Judy, of course. I could hear Pete and Joe whinny every once in a while. I still did not know exactly how Judy had decided to use them.

I was standing in the back of the church ready to escort Grandma Warden to her pew. The church was packed. I gave Grandma and Grandpa a big hug and thanked them. Next was Mrs. Clemons, I held my arm out for her and she didn't take it. So we just walked side by side down the aisle. I gave her a hug when I got her to her pew, I thought I smelled a hint of alcohol.

As I turned back, I saw Mom standing in the back of the church waiting for me. I stood there for a moment, almost paralyzed. Mom was so special. She had done so many years of hard work, yet she was still a lady. Here I was at my own wedding, leading my precious mother down the aisle. After all she had done for me, had I really thanked her enough? I met her in the back of the narthex and I held her. This was my way of thanking her. I looked into her eyes, kissed her forehead, and we then headed down the aisle to her pew with Dad in tow. Harold sang as I walked to the back of the aisle again. Pastor Hanson,

Carl Toney and I made our way up the aisle as Harold finished his song. As I walked up on the main platform, I looked up at the empty cross and thanked Jesus silently.

The processional started. Wade came first with Judy's first cousin, then came Perry with another of Judy's cousins, then came Harold with Becky at his side. They were all smiles. Then came the ring bearer and a flower girl. They were pretty young and very cute. The little guy ended up falling down and started to cry a little. He gathered himself and made his way up to the front eventually. The organist changed over to 'Canon in D' and soon I saw Judy in the back of the church with her dad. The congregation stood as Judy started slowly up the aisle.

I stood there studying every detail as she walked closer to me: her eyes, her lips, her hair, her smile, her beautiful white dress, her veil. She was purely radiant! I'd never seen her this way before. Her eyes pierced me like I was soft butter. Yes, God, this is why you made us male and female. I stepped down and took her hand. She gave me a little hand squeeze and up the few steps we went.

Our ceremony was nothing unusual as far as weddings go, but Judy and I will never forget it. Carl gave the sermon, which made it extra special. We had saved our first kiss on the lips till this day. When Pastor Hanson announced, "You may now kiss the bride," oh boy! The crowd erupted in applause. Harold ended with the Lord's prayer and there were very few dry eyes in the church.

We did the normal reception line, then headed out for a ride in Mr. Olson's hitch wagon with Mr. Olson as our driver, top hat and all. The whole wedding party climbed in and off we went. Laura Molenex surprised us with monarch butterflies to release from little wax paper envelopes right before we left. Pete and Joe were full of themselves, high stepping out of that parking lot at a full trot. Becky had braided them in colors to match the bridesmaids' gowns.

We got back after a short ride and finished up with the pictures that we couldn't take before the wedding. First we took a bunch with the hitch wagon and geldings, and then we took pictures up in the front of church.

Becky asked me, "Jude, do you know how your bride arrived at church before the ceremony?"

"No, but I will guess by the hitch wagon."

"Nope! Ask her."

I looked over to Judy. "Judy?"

"Would you believe I rode in on Pete as Mr. Olson led him to the front of church? It was awesome. Pete was so good!"

We went out and got pictures of Judy riding Pete in and then we surrounded Pete with the whole wedding party as Judy proudly sat on him. It was beautiful, with Judy's white dress draped over Pete's coal black back. Pete was a trooper, standing quietly as we maneuvered about him.

The next stop was Mr. Olson's where we would hitch Pete and Joe to the hitch wagon and drive over to Dad's for the reception with all the wedding party. Mr. Olson had Pete and Joe at their best. We pulled into our driveway with the geldings in step and at a full high-stepping trot. The crowd gave us a standing ovation. We made a few figure eights and stopped by the tent. Cameras clicked like crazy as we sat there in the wagon.

The rest of the reception was great. There was lots of dancing, the roasted hog was superb, the band actually played music you could dance to, and Mr. Olson offered wagon rides.

Judy and I were very blessed on our wedding day with family, relatives, friends, the weather and, of course, Jesus Christ. We flew to Disneyland for our honeymoon. I found myself again thanking God on our honeymoon for making woman. We planned to be newlyweds for the rest of our lives.

Chapter 10
"Life Goes On"

After our honeymoon, we flew back to Minnesota and headed to our very own timberframe home. As we drove in, Pete and Joe were out in the pasture. They raised their heads and trotted our way. Judy and I walked out to greet them as they leaned over the fence.

I was glad to see them again. "How did you boys do when we were gone? Did you miss us?"

Judy hugged them while I scratched their necks. "Pete, I never thanked you for taking me up to the church on my wedding day. That was very special."

As I rubbed on Pete and Joe I looked up toward the front door and an idea popped into my mind. "Judy, let me carry our stuff in and you wait right here till I get back. Okay?"

"Whatever you say, honey. I'll just spoil Pete and Joe some more."

I hustled to the car and carried everything into our home. I walked back to Judy and the geldings and couldn't help staring at Judy's beauty as she conversed with Pete and Joe. I was the luckiest man alive!

"Mrs. Bonner, are you ready to be carried over the threshold of your new home?"

"Mr. Bonner, I would like that very much. Shall we?"

"Why certainly, ma'am." With that I scooped her up in my arms and headed toward the front door.

"Honey, I didn't expect you to carry me the whole way!"

"No problem! In fact, I say we do this on our anniversary every year. Yes ma'am, I promise to stay strong enough for you for many years."

Judy and I went up the front steps and she turned the door knob for us. I stepped over the threshold with the prettiest woman in the world in my arms. I held her and gazed into her eyes. "Judy I love you, and I promise to always take care of you. You are very special to me." I rubbed my nose on hers.

The next few evenings were spent with Judy and I setting up house. All the wedding gifts were on the living room floor, furniture needed to be moved, and Judy had to put her kitchen in place with all the pots and pans.

I'll never forget the night we had visitors just as we were heading to bed. Mom and Dad lined up an old-fashioned shivaree with a bunch of our friends. They dragged us to town and soon Judy was giving me a ride down main street in a wheelbarrow. I had to give her a piggy back ride, and we were both in our pajamas. Next thing we knew we were singing a song from the musical "Oklahoma." I laughed so hard my stomach hurt. What a blessing to have friends and family to keep us on our toes.

Judy was able to get a job at the Paynesville hospital and I was turning customers away with my trimming business. Carl and Dad had warned me about money and marriage. So far I think Judy and I were doing pretty well. We were able to pay extra on our mortgage each month. We also tried to do a date night every two weeks. Judy would be in charge of a surprise destination one week and I would be in charge the next time. We went bowling, biking, horse- back riding, movies, a dinner theater, etc. The next thing we knew we were celebrating our first anniversary, and I even remembered to carry Judy up from the pasture and over the threshold.

That night Judy and I reminisced about our one year of marriage. We took turns talking about quirks and expectations that we experienced in the past year.

Judy went first. "Honey, I'm willing to do it, but please explain why you need your boxers ironed?"

I laughed. "I was going to ask you why you were doing that!"

"Your Mom told me you liked ironed boxers."

"Did it ever cross your mind that Mom was leading you astray? I have never had ironed boxers until we got married." We both laughed.

"Okay, my turn. Can we sleep with the covers not tucked under the foot of the mattress?"

"What! Are you kidding, what's the big deal about that?"

"My feet need more freedom. I can't stand the covers tucked in down there."

"Fine we can try it, but if my feet get cold, you're going to get it. Okay, why do you squeeze the toothpaste tube in the middle, then you leave globs of paste in the sink, along with whiskers after you shave? Honey, you can wash out the sink just as easy as I can."

"I'm sorry Judy, I'm a slob and I promise to improve. How about when I'm sitting on the pot and there are only two squares of toilet paper left and the spare roll is not within reach? When it is getting low, can you place a spare within reach?"

"Fine, fine." Judy conceded. "What is it with you and your dreams?"

"What do you mean?"

"I can't believe how intense they are at times. Hitting me and ripping the covers away?"

"I'm sorry Judy, that's just me. Hopefully it will get better."

Judy was talking about two different nights of dreams for me. The one night I was dreaming there were three rats in our bed down by my feet. I started thrashing my feet trying to get them away from me. I actually stood up and ripped the covers off the bed onto the floor and stood over the bed looking for rats! The next time my dreams interfered with Judy's sleep was when I dreamt I was milking cows and was trying to get a cow up by cupping my hand and slapping the cow on her belly. You guessed it, I was actually slapping Judy on the belly.

"Ya know Judy, I'm the luckiest man in the world! You're so pretty and I'm in love with you."

"Ditto." I carried Judy upstairs.

Soon after our anniversary, my birthday followed. Judy asked what kind of cake I wanted.

"How about a white three layer cake with plenty of brown sugar frosting?"

"That sounds delicious, Jude. I should have thought of that."

That next Saturday I came home from an errand mid morning to find Judy working on my cake. Her three layer cake looked like a giant hamburger! I busted out laughing the second I saw it.

"Hey, let's get a picture of this giant hamburger." You know how in James it talks about the tongue being so powerful, well I sure proved that verse correct. Judy sat there motionless for awhile and then burst into tears.

"Judy, I'm sorry, it's not that big of a deal. I really didn't mean it, it's only a silly cake!"

She walked over to the window and stood there for what seemed an eternity. I slowly walked over to try to console her. I was reaching for her shoulder when she spun around and faced me.

"Jude, am I ever going to be good enough for you!?" She turned away from me.

"Judy, come on you have to under---"

Judy cut me off. "Maybe you should make your own damn cake, if you think you can do better. Ya know, I don't think you have ever forgot the cake I made your family years ago that turned into a disaster. Is that all I am to you, one big failure?" She stormed up to our bedroom. I stood there like an idiot not knowing really what to do. I slowly knelt and asked for God's forgiveness.

"Lord, I'm so sorry! I just hurt one of your daughters and my wife. You gave her to me to love and cherish. I beg your forgiveness and ask your grace to be with Judy right now. Lord I need your guidance to get me through my shortcomings. I pray this to the Holy and Just God, Amen."

I drove back to town and bought some flowers and a card and put them on the kitchen table. That night was spent on the couch for Jude Bonner. I got up early the next morning and made breakfast for my bride. I packed it up on a tray with her flowers and quietly walked upstairs. I lightly knocked on the door. "May I come in?"

I waited a little while and slowly opened the door. Judy lay in bed with her back towards me. I set the tray on the end table and knelt at the edge of the bed.

I said a quick silent prayer and started speaking to Judy. "Yesterday I really hurt the love of my life. I was selfish, stupid, unloving, and full of pride. I humbly ask your forgiveness. I have brought you breakfast in bed as I beg you for a second chance."

I looked up to see if there was any movement or response. She slowly turned in bed and lay there like she was still asleep. I stared into her closed eyes and thought I saw her take a peek at me. I broke into a song from Oklahoma. "Don't say my name too much, don't walk in the rain with me, your hand feels so grand in mine, people will say we're in Love."

Soon Judy's hand was in mine as I sang the next song. "And here I am kneeling here loving you, whether or not I should. I really was a great big jerk!"

Judy lay there trying not to smile. I reached up and gave her a kiss on the lips and sang some more. "Some enchanted morning, you will see a humbled man, you will see a humbled man beside your bed and somehow you'll know, you'll know even then. That somehow you'll forgive him again and again. Once you have married him never let him go, once you have loved him, never let him go!"

"Jude Bonner, how can I stay mad at you when you sing to me like that? I was going to be mad all weekend and teach you a lesson. Hey that breakfast smells pretty good. Let's eat, Buster!"

"Okay sit up and I will serve you."

"Where did you get the flowers, Buster?"

"You see there was a 'Flower Fairy' that knocked on our door last night, knowing I was in big trouble. When I opened the door she had a proposition, I could have the bouquet of flowers if I did the dishes for the next month. So I took her up on her offer."

"Oh Jude, I'm sorry about your cake. I guess I should just buy you a cake from the bakery. So what do you want to do for your birthday today?"

I reached over and gave her another kiss. "How about we saddle up Pete and Joe after church and go for a nice long ride?" It was a great birthday spending it with my bride and Pete and Joe.

Back home at Dad's and Mom's, things were changing. Becky was seeing more and more of Wade Estep. It was only a matter of time before we'd be attending a wedding. Wade was really enjoying the farm life and seemed to be a natural with the cows. Mr. Olson seemed to be slowing down, so Wade spent a fair amount of time over there. Becky had graduated from a two year college with a business management degree and had a good job in Alexandria, Minnesota.

Wedding bells were ringing for Becky and Wade two years after our wedding. They also choose an outdoor reception with Pete and Joe involved. Their new home was at Mr. Olson's. It sure was hard to get used to, but he had decided to move to town and sell his place to Becky and Wade. Their plan was to milk cows and raise kids and Percherons. Mom couldn't wait to be a grandmother. So far God had not blessed Judy and me with children, though we had prayed for them. I tried to convince Judy that we weren't having any luck because she never fixed me baked beans. It was three years into our marriage before I finally realized I never got baked beans. Judy didn't like baked beans so that meant Jude didn't get baked beans.

Yes, life was changing each year. Grandpa Warden passed away from a bad bout of pneumonia. Grandma moved in with Dad and Mom. Becky and Wade had two kids with a third on the way, and though Judy and I were proud of being an aunt and uncle, I had to admit it was frustrating to be childless. It was harder on Judy than on me. She had many heart to hearts with Mom. The doctors couldn't understand why we weren't having any luck, either.

Becky said Mr. Olson came out almost every day to see Ladd and Molly. Molly was bred to a very well-known Percheron stallion and everyone was excited about her foal. Sure enough, ol' Molly delivered a very nice stud colt on Easter morning that year. Mr. Olson was all smiles as he stood there watching that little fella get up for the first time. They named him Geronimo's Black Inferno.

Judy and I spent a lot of time enjoying our nephews. They would spend the night at our place, or we'd take them to Sibley Park exploring. We had so much fun with them. They seemed to be dirt magnets. No puddle could stay calm, no bug left alone. They were a blessing from God.

Judy and I entered our seventh year of marriage and praise God, we were still in love. It was such a privilege to wake in the mornings and pray to the Lord with my wife. In my own prayer time I was asking God for help with Judy's cooking. I'm the worst cook in the world and Judy wasn't far behind me. How could I tell Judy without hurting her feelings? There were times I could barely stomach her meals. I told myself it could be worse.

My youth group was going strong, Judy was in charge of Vacation Bible School at church, and we were both growing in the Lord.

Around this time, I started to feel different physically. I don't know what it was, but I felt off at times. Maybe it was Judy's cooking? I kept thinking it was nothing, so I didn't tell anyone.

In my alone time I did bring my concerns to the Lord, and after that I felt fine for a long time. I thought I was completely over it until I woke up one morning with a horrible taste in my mouth. I gargled with apple cider vinegar and took some antacid. "Oh, it was just something I ate," I said to myself.

That day I had fourteen horses scheduled to trim and I didn't think the day would ever end. I tried to eat lunch but really had no appetite. I felt like a truck had hit me. I had never been so tired in my life. I dragged myself home, took a nice hot bath, and went to bed, sure that in the morning I would feel better. Judy got home late that night so she didn't know how I felt.

Sure enough, the next morning I felt much better. I thanked God during my devotional time and headed off to do chores and trim feet. I still had a funny taste in my mouth, but felt pretty good. I decided I needed to get in better shape and take vitamins. I started a routine of exercise and a few vitamins, which seemed to help a lot. I gained better stamina and had a good appetite. I was on the mend.

Judy was immersed in her work, so much that I felt it was unhealthy for her. She was making extra money with overtime and holiday pay, but at what cost to her or to our marriage? I decided I'd better talk with her soon, so I came home early one afternoon with a grand dinner from the local diner for just the two of us, candlelight and all. Soon Judy walked into the kitchen in her nursing scrubs.

"Do you know how pretty you are, young lady?" I said as I held her in my arms.

"Jude, look at me. If you think this is pretty, I've got news for you." She looked me in the eyes. "What is that I smell, honey? Have you been cooking?"

"You get your butt in the shower, and when you get out, dinner will be served." I gave her a kiss.

I had everything ready to go when Judy got out of the shower. The table was set with dinner rolls, salad, pork roast, sweet corn, baked carrots, and I even had an apple pie in the oven. I had her favorite music on in the background. I met Judy at the bathroom door and escorted her to her chair. We enjoyed a great dinner, and it was such an honor to sit across the table from her and know that she was my wife. I again silently thanked God for making women and marriage.

I cleaned up the kitchen and checked on my pie in the oven.

Soon we were eating warm apple pie a la mode.

I squared up so I was looking Judy right in the eye. "How are things at the hospital?"

"Oh, just fine."

"You seem to be spending more and more time with your job, honey. I'm not sure if that's good for you or us."

Judy looked away from me. I gently grabbed her chin and brought it back to me. "Something is bothering you. Can you please tell me what it is? Did I do something to hurt you?"

I could see the tears starting to form. "It's nothing."

"Judy, we're going to sit here until I hear what's bothering you. Remember our vows, for better or worse, for richer or poorer."

Yes, the tears were full steam ahead now. She folded into my shoulder and just sobbed. I held her and held her. What a privilege.

She eventually blurted out, "Why hasn't God given us children? I'm so sorry, Jude. It must be me. With my past, I guess I can understand. But that's not fair to you."

"I had wondered if this was the problem. 'For men are not cast off by the Lord forever. Though he brings grief, he will show compassion, so great is his unfailing love. For he does not willingly bring affliction or grief to the children of men.' Lamentations 3:31-33."

"I'm so sorry Jude, I'm so sorry. Can you ever forgive me?" she said through her tears.

I sat there and held her very tight, and she finally settled down. "Judy, you need to understand I love you, and I forgive you if you have wronged me which I highly doubt. Children are in God's timing, not ours, and maybe we need to ask God for forgiveness." I ran my finger through her hair. "Now, in the presence of God, let's make sure we give our pasts to him and repent of anything that we think hasn't been brought up before. This will be very hard, but we need to be honest with God and ourselves."

Praise God! Judy sat facing me holding my hands and she poured out her past to me and God that evening. I have to admit it was pretty ugly at times. As I looked into Judy's eyes, I could see the stress leaving and the joy entering again.

I know God had already forgiven Judy of her past, but she needed to voice her past out to me and God for her own healing.

Judy and I prayed to God as a couple and then I took her in my arms and carried her to bed.

"Thank you, Jesus!"

Chapter 11
"Need a New Hobby"

The more I thought about why I was feeling bad at times, the more I figured it had to be stress. So I tried to think of ideas that would relax me and let me unwind. I convinced myself if I could find a new hobby that was relaxing, that would cure all my ills. I was driving down the road one day when I heard an advertisement on the radio for an archery shop in Litchfield. I began thinking about bow hunting. I thought it might be very relaxing sitting in a tree waiting for deer to come by. Besides, my own brother-in-law, Wade, was an avid bow hunter.

That evening at dinner I brought my idea up with Judy. "Honey, I've been thinking about trying some bow hunting. I figure it might help me relax after trimming feet all day, and plus, look at all the time I spent building this house." I scraped my taters together. "What are your thoughts?"

She yawned and stretched. "Not sure?" She got up and sat on my lap. "Maybe I'll let you go if you take me too. But, I suppose you're worried about me outshooting you. I guess I can't blame you for that." She kissed her finger and placed it against my lips.

I started to tickle her and she was soon on the ground incapacitated as we were nose to nose. "So Mrs. Bonner, let's say you do out-shoot me. Who's going to gut and drag your prize home?"

"Oh, that's simple! I'll just harness Pete up. He's way stronger than you." She rubbed her nose on mine and gave me a kiss.

"Besides, if you don't help me, I just might decide to stop cooking for you, you creep."

"Creep!" I tickled her some more. "Let's go to Litchfield on Saturday and see what this might cost us." I lay down beside her. "Why do women always settle disputes with food?" I shook my head.

"That's how God made us. What time are we leaving for our trip to Litchfield?"

"Let's go right after chores. They probably close by noon on Saturdays."

Judy and I made the trip that Saturday to the archery shop in Litchfield. Their shop was fairly new and I couldn't believe how many bows they had. Fred, the owner, helped Judy and me. We had many questions since we really had no experience. He set up a couple bows for us and soon had us shooting arrows in their inside range. Judy was so funny to watch. She would fight to get her bow pulled back and then start laughing as she tried to hold it steady. She shot several arrows where no arrow has ever been before in that range.

"Honey, maybe this wasn't the best idea for me. How about you get a bow and I go with you and take pictures or video?" She rubbed her shoulder as she put her bow down. "My shoulder is killing me!"

"It's up to you. I think this is kind of neat, but you'd better be careful with your shoulder. If you don't get a bow, it would sure save us money."

Fred set up a PSE brand bow for me that I fell in love with. I shot it about thirty times and was starting to get the hang of it. At eleven o'clock we were leaving with a brand new PSE bow with quiver, arrows, release, peep sight, and some camouflage clothing.

As we drove along I was feeling pretty good about my new hobby. "Here's the deal honey, you go out and hunt and I'll go out and take photos. Whoever gets the biggest deer this year, the other one has to do the dishes for a month straight. You in?" She looked my way with a big smile.

"Yes, ma'am."

I ordered books on whitetail hunting while Judy ordered books on wildlife photography. Wade and Becky came over so Wade could help with a few deer stands. We even built the 'Hilton' for Judy to use. It was all boxed in with windows and carpet on the floor and a place for a heater. I wanted to stay with the traditional portable stands you can move from tree to tree. Wade and I practiced shooting together and he gave me pointers. Last year on Dad's property Wade had taken a very nice four and a half year old that scored around one fifty. That one was going on the wall. Summer crept into early fall, and our archery season opened mid September. I was getting all excited to sit in the stand that first evening. Of course, I had everything all planned out in my head; first several small bucks would come by and I would let them go, then a couple does with fawns, then the big boy would mosey in and give me a perfect broadside shot. Yes, sir, this was going to be a piece of cake. Why, I'm surprised I hadn't called the taxidermy guy up in Osakis and set up an appointment with the meat locker in Belgrade!

There I was, sitting in my best spot the evening of the opener for archery. I could barely see Judy across the meadow in the "Hilton" with her camera. By the time this evening was over, Judy would be doing dishes for the next month. It wasn't long and here they came. I couldn't believe how many were coming out, and so soon. Not deer, but MOSQUITOES!

Wade had warned me about early season hunting with bugs, but I was different, they wouldn't bother me, they wouldn't be that bad. I sat there trying my best to hold still as mosquitoes made a pin cushion out of me. I swear their ring leader buzzed by my ears the whole night. I looked across the way and knew Judy was doing fine in her screened in "Hilton." My whole focus was on the mosquitoes and I was asking God why he created such an insect. It was the last straw when one of them flew up my nose to do some exploring. I put my finger on my left nostril and started blowing him out the right nostril. The inside of my nostril itched like crazy so I was rubbing it and blowing it back and forth.

When I finally got my nose back into shape, I looked up and there he stood looking at me. Mr. Antler, the biggest buck I'd ever seen! I felt like an idiot. How long had he been standing there? He was only twenty yards away. I strained to look at my bow hanging to my right. Could I grab it without spooking the big boy? He started to shake his head and rubbed his nose with his right front leg, snorted and then trotted off toward the "Hilton." I sat there in disbelief. That did not just happen! I shook my head. Was that deer mimicking me with his head shake and leg to the nose rub and snorting?

I sat there till dusk watching "Mr. Antler" munching on the clover near Judy's stand. I quietly gathered my things, climbed down, and made my way back home with my tail between my legs. I have to believe every mosquito in the county was following me, along with a few deer flies. As I walked along the edge of the bean field, I heard the ping on my cell phone.

Sure enough, it was Judy. "I'll probably be late deer (get it), the deer you couldn't handle is giving me tons of nice pictures. You might start the dishes when you get home, luv you!"

I had to admit, that was funny. I was running that scene of "Mr. Antler" through my mind while walking home. The "what if" list got bigger with each step. I'll bet I made up ten excuses I could tell Judy when she got home. When I got home, I stood in front of the sink convincing myself I had to do dishes, not so sure this new hobby was taking stress away.

I was just finishing the last dish when Judy snuck in the back door. She slipped in behind me and gave me a hug. "What a great evening to be out in God's creation! It was so relaxing just sitting there and taking shots of that big buck. It's like he was posing for me the whole time. Oh, by the way, did you have any luck tonight, honey?"

I turned and faced my lovely wife. "My dearest lady, my luck was a little different than yours. First I was attacked by a million skeeters, second I was mocked by 'Mr. Antler,' and third, I had to do all these dishes." I gave her a big kiss. "Now let's see those pictures you took of Mr. Antler."

"What's this Mr. Antler stuff? I named him 'Bubba.' Now until you can get the job done, we'll call him Bubba."

"Whatever you say, my Princess. Let's see how your pictures turned out."

We put the disk in our computer and were soon was looking at 'Bubba' from all angles. Bubba was quite the specimen. He was a main frame eleven pointer with lots of kickers all over the place! We emailed them over to Wade. Soon the phone was ringing.

"Hello."

Wade hammered out the questions. "Jude, that deer is a pig! What a monster! I'll bet he'll make Boone & Crockett, my goodness. Did he get close to your stand at all, or was he just by Judy's?"

I stalled a little, trying to come up with an excuse. "First of all, mosquitoes ate me alive, second, a mosquito flew up my nose, and third, Bubba played me for a fool!"

"Do I hear that male ego kicking in here junior? Kind of tough when your wife out hunts a guy! Maybe I need to come over and show you how it's done." Wade then sneezed right into the phone.

"Thanks Wade. I've gotta regroup here and hopefully Bubba gives me a second chance. See ya later."

Needless to say, that night I lay there thinking of all the ways to get a shot at Bubba. Of course, all my ways had me hanging him on the wall of our living room. Yes, I had the bug. All I could think of was Bubba and his beautiful rack. One thing for sure is Jude was not going out again till the bugs got better.

About two weeks later, my phone was ringing just as I was finishing my day of trimming feet. It was Becky. "Jude, you got a minute?"

"Sure."

"Can you do us a favor?"

"Maybe, what is it?"

"Wade and I have a chance to get away for a weekend and we're wondering if you and Judy would watch the kids."

"I'll have to check with Judy, but I assume we can handle that. When is this going to happen?"

"The weekend of October tenth."

"I'll check with Judy tonight and let you know. Gotta go, bye."

Soon Judy and I were in charge of three pork chops for the weekend: Nancy, five years old, Jeff, three years old, and Troy, twenty months old. Wow, does that ever put a different perspective on life! It was, "Uncle Jude can we do this?" and "Aunt Judy can we do that?" Jeff was at the "why" stage of life. Every statement Judy or I made was followed by "why." It's hard to believe we all went through that same step in life.

Judy and I were loving every minute of their stay. I can't even count how many times we read the same book to them over and over. And how about hide-n-seek with the younger ones only hiding behind their hands? I became Pete, and had to give them rides on my back until my knees were killing me. Nancy was into dress up and soon I was dancing with a little princess, while Jeff and Troy were all tractors and trucks. You can see at an early age how God created girls and boys differently.

It was chore time and we decided to take the kids out to see Pete and Joe. We bundled them up and headed outside to work with three little "pork chops." Their version of work was way different from ours. I had to continually remind myself to walk slower, as they were walking like little kids with stubby little fat legs.

Pete and Joe saw us from a distance and whinnied loudly, thundering across the pasture to greet us. I had to laugh. Pete and Joe could care less about Judy and I, they were only interested in the kids. They stretched their massive heads over the gate and greeted Nancy, Jeff, and Troy. At first the kids were apprehensive, but they soon started giving Pete and Joe head hugs. The geldings were so gentle with them. Joe would nuzzle Troy till he slowly fell over and he'd get back up only to have Pete do the same thing again. Judy gave each of the kids an apple treat to give them. Troy wasn't so sure. I think he wanted to eat it himself. We moved on to our other chores and when finished realized that chores took three times as long with our special company. We lost track of how many "why" questions we got from Jeff.

After chores, Judy started supper while I played blocks with the pork chops. Becky forgot to tell me we would be eating cheesy mac, not exactly my favorite. Out of the mouths of babes was next on the agenda. We said our table prayers and Judy was scooping out the cheesy mac.

It was dead silent when Jeff casually looked over to Troy and said, "You and I have a penis." Of course that got my attention and flew right over Troy's head.

Jeff looked away a few seconds and looked back to Troy. "Aunt Judy and Faith, they don't have one." I sat there biting my lip, looking at Jeff.

He looked at me and said, "You've got one too!" Thank the Lord for that. I gave Judy a quick glance and noticed a slight smile on her face.

Nancy must have figured she needed to comment on this anatomy class. She looked at Judy and quietly said, "Mom and I don't have one, but we're not sure if Dad knows that."

Judy could hardly hold it in. "Okay kids, it's time to eat."

After supper it was bath time and more book time and then off to bed. Bath time was quite the experience, water everywhere. I couldn't believe how those little porkers came up with all the excuses of not going to bed. They were thirsty, they needed one more book, they were hungry, it was too early, they had more prayers... .

God had another surprise for Judy and me with a major thunderstorm. We lay in bed and soon heard the pitter-patter of little bare feet headed our way. Nancy and Jeff were scared of the storm. Troy slept right through it. You guessed it, I had the privilege of four little feet in my face and back that whole night. I lay there and thanked Jesus for little kids!

We had several killing frosts after the kids left, so most of the bugs would be dead. It was time to put some time in the tree stand waiting for Bubba. While walking to the stand, I told myself I needed redemption from my last time with Bubba. Judy was in the Hilton with her little heater, while the real man was strapped to an Ash tree. The wind was about twenty miles per hour from the west with a temp of twenty degrees, and I soon found out I didn't have enough layers of clothes on. The air cut through me like a knife. I zipped my jackets up all the way, pulled my hat on, and hunkered down. I kept telling myself that this was my night to put Bubba down. God kept telling me I was freezing to death. My toes were beyond cold, my fingers could barely move, and I was starting to shiver a little.

I looked at my phone to see what time it was and I still had one and a half hours of shooting time left. I sat there trying to convince myself I could do this, I was a man! I curled up as much as I could trying to stay warm. I was now shivering uncontrollably and could barely feel my fingers. I looked at my phone a second time only to find I had one hour and twenty-five minutes of shooting time left.

My hands were so cold I almost dropped my cell phone getting it back to my pocket. I looked up and there was Bubba heading my way! I slowly stood up and grabbed my bow with my frozen fingers. The closer he got, the more I shook. Was it from the cold or was I getting buck fever? The wind was blowing right in my face as I tried to attach my release to the bow string. Bubba kept right on walking like I wasn't even there. I raised my bow with my eyes all watery from the wind. I couldn't see anything through the peep sight! I wiped my tears with my sleeve and refocused my attention on Bubba as he kept on walking. If I had any chance of a good shot, I needed to stop him with a little grunt of my voice. I pursed my frozen lips and tried to give Bubba my best grunt. I soon found out I was too cold to produce any sound. Bubba walked out of bow range as I stood there shivering like a mad man. He did stop and look my way for about two seconds, then continued on toward the Hilton.

I was too cold to even get mad. I could barely function to gather my things and undo my safety harness. It seemed like everything took forever to do. I didn't think I would ever get my feet on the ground again. I carefully lowered myself down the tree one step at a time. When I got on the ground I could see Bubba's silhouette near the Hilton. The muscles in my legs were fighting me every step of the way home. I hadn't been this cold since driving Pete and Joe through that blizzard when Mr. Olson had his heart attack. My phone pinged as I walked, but I was too cold to mess with that at the time. I'm sure it was Judy starting the jabs already.

When I got to the back door I could barely turn the door knob to get in. I slipped in and sat down to untie my boot laces. My fingers were not cooperating. With boots finally off, I ran to the living room and just about hugged our wood stove. It was now my best friend. I held my hands above the warm stove trying to absorb all the heat it would give me. Next came the pain of frozen to warmth. Why it hurts, I don't know, but the pain was worth it. Besides, I always tell Judy and Mom that men can take pain. I peeled outer layers of clothing off and was starting to feel like a human again. That's when I heard the calling. The dishes in the sink were calling my name.

It took some talking on my part, but I finally walked over and started the dishes. Actually, the warm water felt good on my fingers. I heard the back door open. How could I counter Judy's response this time? I dried my hands and thought. The only thing I could think of was singing "Go away little Girl" as I leaned against the sink watching Judy head my way. Soon Judy and I were dancing as I sang into her ear. I swooped her up in my arms and carried her upstairs.

Three weeks later was the night Bubba and I would meet at the pass. We had six inches of fresh snow on the ground, about thirty-five degrees, and no wind. I was pumped. With the new snow, I was able to walk to my stand unannounced. I got all settled in my stand and sat back and took in all of God's beauty before me. The blue jays swooped in and out of the ditch bank as they split the cool air with their piercing calls. An ermine in his snow white winter coat ran on a tree branch that was on the ground. He would stop and look around and then dive into the reed canary grass and disappear for a few seconds. His movements soon caught the attention of the blue jays. The jays were dive bombing him from all angles. He would duck and run, wondering what happened to his world. He would side step one Jay only to have two others swooping in from his back side. He scurried up the tree beside me looking for a safe place as the jays were right on his tail. Sure enough, he found a hole in the side of the tree and quickly climbed in. It was very entertaining to sit there and watch his little head pop out of the hole to see if the coast was clear. The jays soon lost interest and he went back down to the ground and headed north. I sat there and thanked Jesus for allowing me to take in His wonderful creation.

It was so quiet out there that I was lulled into a trance. All of a sudden, out of the corner of my eye, something was heading my way, and very fast. I sat at attention. It was a sharp shinned hawk, thinking my eyes were his supper. He got about five feet from my face and realized I was a little bigger than he could handle. He put the brakes on in mid air and shot to the left as fast as he could. He landed in a Hackberry tree forty yards away and kept his eye on me the rest of the night. I gazed at him through my binoculars, then scanned the ditch line for Bubba. Yes sir, there he was, working a scrape on an Ironwood sapling south of me.

I hung the binos up and got myself ready. This time I had all the pieces in place. My heart was throbbing in my chest and my mouth was cotton dry as Bubba headed my way at a trot. I couldn't take my eyes off his rack. He looked bigger than before! With the snow in the background, he seemed all that more magnificent. He stopped a couple times and scanned the horizon for predators and to test the wind. From what I could tell, he was on a mission to walk right in front of me.

I had picked out several lanes where I could grunt at him to stop him for a good shot. I was believing my own press and was convinced this was a cake walk. He was getting closer. I slowly raised my bow and got ready. At twenty yards broadside he stopped in my first, and best, shooting lane. I started to pull the bow back, but it had other ideas. What was going on? I couldn't pull the string back! Bubba walked over to my next shooting lane and stood broadside again.

I was doing mental gymnastics. Could I pull the bow back, would Bubba stand there, and how far would he go after my arrow hit his vitals? Bubba was starting to get nervous and twitching his tail. It was now or never. I put all my strength into pulling that string back. At first it was a stalemate. I changed my approach with a big arched pull and gradually gained ground. Things were looking better. Bubba's massive rack would soon be in my hands for pictures. Halfway drawn my index finger slipped onto the release and my arrow flew through the sky like the arch of one of God's rainbows. I couldn't believe it! I'll bet that arrow shot above Bubba by twenty feet in the air. Bubba twitched his tail, looked up at me, and rubbed his nose with his front foot again. I stood there like an idiot as Bubba trotted off towards the Hilton.

That was the longest walk home in my life. Maybe I wasn't cut out for this.

Chapter 12
"The Barn Service"

The aftermath of our new hobby was very prominent in our home. Judy had several of her best photos framed and hung in our home. Yes, every day I was able to see the deer that made a fool out of me. God must be telling me something. I did keep my part of the bargain and did dishes for most of that winter.

The closer we got to Christmas that year the more I was thinking about a special service for Christmas Eve. I talked with God about it and lay in bed at night thinking of details. One night as Judy lay beside me, she asked, "Jude, you got something stirring in that brain of yours. When you going to let me in on it?"

"Why do you say that?"

"Eyes open, staring at the ceiling, very little movement, those are signs of Jude Bonner master-minding something." She started laughing. "I just hope it is better than your deer hunting scheme."

"Judy, you must admit, if I hadn't thought of deer hunting, you never would have gotten pictures of Bubba." I looked her way and gave her a kiss. "I'm thinking of two events, one is your Christmas gift, and what do you think of having a Christmas Eve service in the barn this year?"

She looked my way with a small smile on her face. "That sounds kind of neat, especially the part about my gift. Tell me more."

"Imagine, ten o'clock on Christmas Eve, hay bales for seating, Pete and Joe in their tie stalls, some chickens, calves, and most important, an empty manger waiting for baby Jesus."

"Oh Jude, that sounds so cozy. Who would come?"

"We leave that part for God. We would sing a bunch of carols, have special readings, and maybe hitch Pete and Joe afterward for a midnight sleigh ride."

"Speaking of hitching Pete and Joe, you promised we would get a live tree this year. Could we hitch Pete and Joe to get our Christmas tree? We need to do that soon. And by the way, I'm still waiting for the part about my present."

"Maybe I'll give you a hunk of coal for Christmas this year!" I rubbed my nose on hers. "How about this Saturday? I'll get the bobsled out and ready this week, and off we'll go. I want to get a big tree this year!"

Late that Saturday morning, Judy, Pete, Joe and I were heading south with our bobsled, rope, hand saw, and high spirits. We lived two miles from a cut your own Christmas tree farm. We pulled into their lot and had many looks as Pete and Joe made their way through the rows of pines. We made several passes and found what I thought was the perfect tree.

"Jude, don't you think it's a little too big?"

"It'll look great right by the stairs, honey. Yup, this is the one. It has our name on it!"

I got down and grabbed the hand saw and starting crawling under the lower branches. Wow! The ground was covered in coon crap on that side. I crawled back out to go to the other side.

"What's wrong Jude?"

"Yuck, there is some nasty stuff on that side on the ground."

"I still think it is too big."

"It'll be fine honey, I've got things under control."

I was soon sawing away at the base of the tree. I stopped to rest and Pete started to nicker. Then I saw someone hugging Pete's leg. "Judy, are you watching Pete?"

"Kelly, how are you doing?" Judy asked.

I was trying my best from under the tree to figure out who Kelly was. "Who is it, Judy?"

"It's Kelly from the fair. She still remembers Pete."

"Hi Kelly, how you doing? We haven't seen you for years." I shouted from under the tree.

In her Down Syndrome voice she quietly said. "I fine. I miss Pete."

I went back to sawing as Kelly and Pete talked back and forth.

It would have helped if I had a sharp saw. Next thing I knew, the saw was bound up. I crawled back out and pushed on it only to have the wind bring it back onto the saw. Kelly's dad came to my rescue and held it so the saw was free again. I soon had our White Spruce on the ground beside the bobsled. With the help of Kelly's dad we got it loaded and tied down. Kelly's parents took some pictures of Kelly, Judy and I with our very first live Christmas tree.

You could see the excitement in Kelly as she looked up at me. "Mr. Bonna, don't you tink tree too big?"

I gave a quick glance over to Judy. "Kelly, it will be fine. Do you want to come over and help us decorate the tree today?"

Kelly got a huge gleam in her eye and gave me a hug. She looked toward her parents. "Mom, I go with Pete and Joe?"

Yes sir, Pete and Joe not only had to haul the tree back home, but Kelly was front and center with a grin as big as a barn. I even let her hold the reins when we got out in the field. When we got home, I pulled up by our front porch, took Pete and Joe into the barn, untied the tree, and started dragging it up the steps toward the front door. I had to admit it was looking kind of big.

We lined the door jams with heavy cardboard to make it easier to pull through. Kelly and Judy helped me pull it through the front door. The tree was starting to win the battle. We started counting to three and all pulled together. I was starting to get mad and tried all the harder. Yep, I soon had a tree stuck in our front door. I tried pushing it back out but it was not going anywhere. I stood there fuming. I knew what Judy was thinking, so I dared not look her way.

The place was dead quiet until Kelly spoke up. "Mr. Bonna, tree too big."

Judy burst out laughing immediately followed by Kelly. I caught my anger rising at first, but Kelly was right, the tree was too big! I looked at Kelly and couldn't help busting out laughing with them. I think we all had tears running down our cheeks.

"Okay Kelly, maybe you're right. The tree might be too big." We all laughed some more. "Kelly, let's go. You lead Pete out of the barn while I get a rope and a single tree. Meet me by that window."

Judy was filming as Kelly proudly led Pete up to the window. I went inside and tied my end of the rope to the base of the tree and then opened the window and threw the extra to Kelly. I crawled out the window and tied the other end to the single tree.

"Kelly, please step back a little while I lead Pete forward." I held Pete by his halter. "Okay Pete, easy boy, let's go." Pete took the slack out of the rope and stopped. I tugged some on his halter. "Come on Pete, let's go." Pete leaned into the collar and started slowly moving forward while I held his halter. Hey, this was working great. I looked back at Kelly to get her approval, and the next thing I knew I was tripping over a two foot tall Blue Spruce we had planted for our fifth anniversary.

I went down while Pete's head went up with steeled eyes. I almost lost my grip. Pete side stepped quickly while I struggled to get my feet under me again. Pete was gaining speed as I hollered, "Whoa!" I finally could dig my heals into the ground and pull back on Pete's halter. Just before I got him stopped, I heard a big thud from inside the house. I looked back at the window and could see lots of Spruce branches.

Pete was prancing and all nervous as I stood there thinking of the possible damage I just did to our home. I shook my head in disgust and then noticed Kelly crying. Judy headed over to console her while I unhooked Pete from the rope.

I led Pete over to them as Judy held Kelly. "I sorry Mr. Bonna, I sorry Mr. Bonna, I sorry…" Kelly kept repeating while huge tears streamed down her face.

I didn't know what to do. I didn't know what to say. Why did Kelly think this was her fault? I looked at Judy and she gave me a bewildered look back.

Fighting my own tears, I tried to talk with Kelly. "Kelly, you did nothing wrong at all, this whole episode was totally my fault. Kelly, I'm so sorry if I hurt you in any way."

"Please don't beat Pete, don't beat him Mr. Bonna. Can you take me home?" Kelly was hysterical. Why would she think I was going to beat Pete? I was overcome with emotion. I let go of the lead rope and began wiping my own tears.

Pete slowly made his way over to Kelly. I looked up through my tears and watched Pete push Kelly with his massive head. She clung all the tighter to Judy. I think she thought it was me pushing her. Pete stepped back and nickered softly and then nudged her again.

When Kelly looked up and saw it was Pete, she let go of Judy and clung to Pete's front leg. There they stood, Kelly wrapped around Pete's chest, his head against her back. Kelly was still crying as Pete's chest grew wet with her tears. I truly believe the bond between Pete and Kelly was stronger than my bond with Pete. I was okay with that. I bowed my head and thanked our heavenly Father for allowing me to witness His grace and mercy.

After wiping many tears, Judy and I made our way into the house to check out the damage. Yes, the tree that was too big now had punched a hole through the sheetrock below the window. I think Judy was laughing under her breath as she inspected the damage. We both looked out the window and saw Pete following Kelly to the barn. I spun the tree around and started cleaning the mess up.

Kelly came in the front door after putting Pete in the pasture. "Mr. Bonna, tank you for not beating Pete. He my friend."

"Kelly, I would never beat Pete. What happened today was totally my fault." I put my arm around her. "Can you tell me why you would think I would hurt Pete?"

She started crying again and spoke between gasps of air. "That's what my Grandpa would do to my horse every time something went wrong." She was really losing it again. "He whipped my best buddy, Silver, with barbed wire right in front of me one day!"

Of course I was crying again. "Kelly, I'm so sorry. I never would have guessed." I softly grabbed her chubby little chin and looked her in the eyes. "Kelly, I promise never to hurt Pete or Joe or any horse, and I never have. How bout I fix you a cup of hot chocolate?" She shook her head ''yes'' as Judy came to hold her.

I whipped up three cups of hot chocolate with marshmallows in each one and brought them out on a tray. Kelly was getting her composure back and seemed glad to hold her cup. I had to laugh as it seemed like Kelly had more on her face than she drank, but she was happy again and that was all that mattered.

With Kelly's help we hoisted the tree up in its spot and started decorating with lights and tinsel and all sorts of ornaments. We had Christmas music going on the CD player and snacks to munch on. Kelly's version of hanging ornaments was quite unique. She would hang several really close together, then leave a gap and hang another bunch super close together. When we were all done, we sat on the couch together drinking hot cocoa and admiring our handy work.

"Kelly, this has to be the best Christmas Judy and I have ever had. Thank you for helping." Kelly had her huge chocolate smile on again. What a privilege to be around someone so genuine. Judy and I drove her home and sang carols the whole time. After we dropped her off we sat at the end of their driveway and thanked our Lord and Savior for that special day.

"Jude, Kelly is so special. We were blessed, so blessed. We need to make sure they get invited to the barn service," said Judy

Next our energy went into planning a Christmas Eve Barn Service. Judy got hold of some of the neighbors and they agreed to help. We sent out an invite on Facebook, and soon our phones were constantly ringing with offers for help and simple questions. The weather would be a big factor since the barn had no heat.

Judy was the organizer of the two of us, and she soon had a theme for the service and readings to support it. She even thought of a skit that some kids could do. The excitement built the closer we got to Christmas Eve.

That morning I set up hay bales for the seating and added some temporary lighting so people could read their music. Judy made the brown paper bags with sand and candles for lighting the way. Judy and I sat in the house waiting for ten o'clock to finally arrive. By nine, we both headed toward the barn to set up the candles and curry out Pete and Joe.

We couldn't believe it when headlights started coming up the driveway at a quarter after nine. It was our neighbors, the VanDerstools, coming to help: Ma, Pa, kids, and their dog, Brandy. I hoisted a kid up on each horse and put them to work on the manes. Pete and Joe seemed curious as to what all the fuss was about.

The weather was not cooperating a whole lot. It was ten degrees with a strong wind out of the east. More and more headlights were coming up the driveway. We soon had about forty people seated on hay bales. Most brought blankets to wrap up in to stay warm. The VanDerstools' dog, Brandy, had to work the crowd to make sure everyone had a chance to pet her. She stuck her face right into each person's face and tried to lick them. I stood back and watched how the people reacted to Brandy.

It was just a couple minutes before starting time when our head pastor, Ken Wolbeck, strolled in with his wife and two young daughters, Laura and Alyssa. The only place left open was right up front next to Pete and Joe's flanks. I was standing right behind the geldings getting ready to start our first ever Christmas Eve Barn Service. The crowd was getting settled in and Judy gave the nod to start the service.

"I'd like to welcome you all to our barn service this glorious night."

I paused for just a second as the place was dead quiet, when all of the sudden little Alyssa nudged her dad with her elbow and asked, "What's that?" pointing to the plumbing on the under sides of Pete and Joe. All eyes fell on pastor Wolbeck, wondering how he was going to explain this to little Alyssa.

Ken looked at me for counsel and I could only smile and shrug my shoulders. "Well honey, that's how you tell if this is a boy horse or girl horse." He looked back at me with a sigh of relief on his face.

All attention was on the Wolbecks as everyone wanted see how a pastor would handle this impromptu anatomy lesson.

Soon it was Laura's turn. "So these are girl horses?"

Ken shook his head a little and answered very quickly so it could end. "Yes."

Well, Mrs. Wolbeck had different ideas. "Oh no, these are both boy horses!"

Judy caught my eye and suggested to keep things rolling. "Let's sing 'Joy to the World,' number nine on your sheets." I announced.

The service was progressing very well with the skit and the readings. Brandy was laying by some other little sleeping kid. We were in the middle of singing "We Three Kings" when Pete reached over and ripped Mrs. Wolbeck's sheet music out of her hand. I hustled over there and got it back for her, horse slobber and all. I had to wonder, if we ever did this again, would Pastor Ken and his family come back?

We finished the service with "Silent Night" and Brandy howling along. It was too cold to hitch the horses, so some people went home after the service and some came up to our house for hot chocolate and cookies.

It was 11:45 PM by the time the last family left for home. After I closed the door, I turned and picked up Judy and carried her under the mistletoe. "Thank you for being the best wife in the world for me. I'm so blessed to have married you. Now, tell me what you got me for Christmas or I won't kiss you."

"In fifteen minutes it will be Christmas. Should we open gifts so you can find out?"

"Oh no way, Becky and I talked Mom and Dad into that one

year. It ruined our Christmas! We woke the next morning with all the pizzazz gone. I'll never forget that. Now, what did you get me?"

"You creep, kiss me and carry me upstairs. You'll have to wait till morning to see what I got you. I think you'll like it."

Judy and I kissed under the mistletoe and I carried her upstairs. "Young lady, here you go calling me a creep and I still carry you upstairs. I don't get it."

Judy looked me in the eyes as we went up. "Yes God! I'm in love with a creep, thank you Lord."

Before I went to sleep that night, I asked God to get me up early so I could fix breakfast for Judy. Five thirty Christmas morning I awoke, slipped out of bed quietly, got dressed and headed out for chores. Pete and Joe were waiting for me by the tractor tire we used as a hay feeder. Of course, Joe had to slip his nose near mine as I put the bale in. "Joe, you big dummy, Merry Christmas!" I lightly blew into his nostril.

The timing was perfect. Wade's truck came up the drive as I walked to the house. Out popped Dad, Mr. Olson and Wade. We had work to do! Judy's present was in the back and it was very heavy. We muscled it in the back door to the utility room.

"Thanks guys, Merry Christmas!"

I got back into the house, cooked up breakfast eggnog and all, and headed upstairs. I stood near the bed and admired my wife sleeping, all snuggled in. I decided to sing her awake. "Sometimes in the morning when you are asleep, I lie here beside you just watching you sleep. And just for a moment that I'm dreaming of my cup runneth over with love. Merry Christmas, honey bunch. Breakfast is served."

Judy yawned and stretched. "Singing and breakfast, I might have to keep you around for a long time. This looks so good. Merry Christmas honey."

I gave her a big kiss. "Last night I was a 'creep' now I'm 'honey.' What gives?"

We ate breakfast while the sun snuck in our east window. The eggnog was ice cold and so thick you almost had to chew it. I drank several glasses that morning. "Jude, you're going to get sick if you drink too much of that eggnog. How can you drink so much at one time? Okay, after breakfast you need to stay up here while I put something under the tree." Judy commanded. "Then I'll come back up and you can carry me back down."

"Hey, what is this? I think you're taking advantage of me!"

"You love it and you know it! Now wait here and I'll be back."

Soon I was carrying my lovely bride back downstairs. I couldn't wait to see what was under the tree that was new. There were two long and flat packages wrapped in newspaper. We always opened stockings first, then our bigger presents next.

We take turns opening so it lasts longer. We each got the usual stuff: gloves, hooded sweat shirt, undies, socks, etc.

Judy stood up and gave me a big hug and a kiss. "Now you sit down and I'll get your gifts from under the tree."

The paper crinkled as she brought them over to me and sat them on my lap. "Am I allowed to guess?"

"Absolutely not! Now open them before I do."

I peeled back paper and looked at two pairs of brand new snowshoes, bindings and all. "Wow Judy! These are nice, great idea!" I slowly ran my hands up and down them. "Where did you get them?"

"Santa's shop at the north pole, where else!" She gave me a big kiss. "Do you like them?"

"Why certainly, why certainly. I say we try them out today! How about I pick up some of this paper while you get us some fudge from the utility room?"

Judy hesitated a little and walked toward the utility room. "Okay?"

I'm sure Judy was wondering where her present was. She was about to find out. I silently followed her to see her reaction.

"Jude Bonner! You creep!" I peeked around the corner as she sat on the piano bench and softly touched the ivory keys.

I walked in and wrapped my arms around my young bride. "Merry Christmas. I love you."

I sat down beside her as she sat there closing and opening the door for the keys. Then she stood up and lifted the lid to see inside. "Oh Jude, this is so beautiful! How did you know I wanted one?"

"One of Santa's elves came to me and told me. Now are you going to sit down and tickle those keys or not?"

"But I haven't played for years."

"It's like riding a bike. Have you looked in the bench?"

Judy started pushing me off the bench and slowly opened the lid. "Jude, this is too good to be true. Music books and piano lessons for a year. I think I'm going to cry."

"Some day when I get old, I'll just lay there and you can serenade me with some love songs. Now I say we go out and try them snowshoes you bought and then come in and move this piano into the spare room."

Sadness briefly flashed across Judy's face when I mentioned the spare room. It was her hope that it would be filled with a child by now. "Carry me upstairs so we can get ready for snowshoeing, you creep. I love you, thank you so much."

We kissed all the way up the stairs. Thank you Lord!

Chapter 13
"Night of Martyrs"

Snowshoeing on Christmas Day was very special. We saw pheasants, deer, wild turkeys, and one mink. It took awhile to get used to walking in the shoes. We each fell down a couple times. I tell ya, it's hard getting back up with snowshoes on. Judy's right shoe came off and I had to help her get it back on. But walking in virgin snow is really neat, so quiet.

The longer we walked, the more my stomach started churning. Yes, the eggnog was brewing up a storm, and I was a long way from our bathroom. I talked myself into believing I could make it back home before having to use the bathroom. But that eggnog had different ideas, and my stomach was screaming for relief. I doubled over in pain and held my gut.

"Did somebody drink too much eggnog, honey?" Judy said with a slight edge to her voice.

"Oh, it's not that. I'll be fine. In fact when we get home I think I'll have a big glass of ice cold eggnog. Did you know that after the birth of Jesus, eggnog is second on the list of Christmas happenings. Mary and Joseph fed baby Jesus eggnog."

"Jude Bonner, can you show me that in the Bible?"

"You betcha! It's in Hesitations 1:6." My stomach was now in full throttle as I was lying to Judy. "I think I need to go talk with that big Ash tree over there, Judy. Can you please excuse me, ma'am?"

I did the "curly" shuffle over to that tree as quick as I could. I barely made it. Wow, that was close! Squatting by an Ash tree on Christmas Day was not on my bucket list.

I sheepishly made my way back to Judy as she patiently waited on an old stump. I still felt like a truck had just run me over.

"I hope everything came out okay. When we get back let's have a huge glass of eggnog and a big piece of fudge. What do you think?"

Ouch, just the thought of eggnog almost made me puke! "I think I'll pass."

We got back into the house, had some hot chocolate by our fireplace, and stared at our beautiful Christmas tree. "Jude, this was one of my favorite Christmases, with Kelly helping decorate, you pulling the tree through the house with Pete, and taking in God's creation snowshoeing."

"Hey, those snowshoes were a great gift. What made you think of that?"

"Never mind that! What made you go out and buy me a piano?" Judy laughed.

"I remember seeing one at your house in the basement. I knew your parents didn't play, and I've seen you at church kind of hanging around the piano. I hope to learn to play from you."

After lunch, Judy sat down to her piano and pecked out a few songs she remembered from when she took lessons as a kid. I lay on the couch just listening. It is probably my favorite musical instrument. That evening we did our traditional movie for Christmas, "It's a Wonderful Life." We snuggled on the couch and cried together like a couple of little kids as the movie ended. And yes, I had to carry Judy up to bed.

The rest of that winter was fairly nice: above average temps and very little snow. Youth group was going well, the kids were anxious for spring. I started planning with my adult leaders a spring event. I had read about it in a Christian teen magazine. It was called "The Night of Martyrs." It revolved around the early church years when Christians had to sneak to secret churches or get persecuted by soldiers who were out looking for them.

The adult leaders were getting excited about it so we presented it to the kids. A few of the parents were asked to help provide soldiers, jail keepers, etc. I lay in bed one night re-thinking the whole deal and a thought came to me. What if Pete and Joe were involved? That thought got stuck in my mind and all I could think of was how to use Pete and Joe during the event. I soon had it all figured out as the clock showed 2:30 AM.

The next morning I presented my case to Judy. "I'm thinking of using Pete and Joe for the Night of Martyrs event. What do you think?"

"How would you use them for that night?"

"We would move it to a night with a full moon so we'd have some natural light. We could have two riders, Kelly and I, dressed as soldiers patrolling the grounds and escorting the kids back to jail. We could order costumes for Pete and Joe so they would look like War Horses. The more I think about it, the better I like it."

"I suppose you spent half the night dreaming that up. I've got to get to work. Just keep safety in mind for the kids and Pete and Joe. Love you, bye." She gave me a kiss and left for work.

I presented my horse idea to the adult leaders and they all liked it. We watched the calendar and scheduled it for April 20th, a Saturday night. We made some simple crosses, bought some cheap soldier costumes on the net, and cleaned up our barn for the jail. We asked the local appliance stores to save us their big cardboard boxes for remote churches. We prayed for good weather and no clouds, along with God's will to be done.

The morning of the event, I gathered some firewood for our fire that was going to simulate burning Christians on the crosses we made. I was very excited and full of adrenaline and going strong, but as I worked I started to feel kind of blah. I knelt down and prayed. "Lord Jesus, you are the I Am. I ask for your blessing on this night. Bring your hand upon us with safety and good weather. Lord, give me your words to say in your timing as I present your gospel. If it's in your will Lord, I could use some help with my health. I pray this through the Lord Jesus Christ, Amen."

I looked at my cell phone clock as Kelly's parents pulled up the drive with Kelly two hours early. She jumped out of her car and seemed ready for action. "Kelly how you doing? Are you ready to chase some Christians?"

"Yup, Mr. Bonna! I hope not too late."

I had to laugh under my breath a little. "No Kelly, you're not too late. And when are you going to call me Jude instead of Mr. Bonner? That makes me feel old. How about you get the geldings in the barn and clean them up."

Kelly was off to the pasture to round up Pete and Joe while

I took the cardboard boxes around and placed them in various places. When I got back, Kelly had the geldings all cleaned up and ready for the big night. Her eyes shown like big diamonds as she lightly touched the bright colored cloth of the costumes for Pete and Joe. She looked up at me with her one of a kind smile. "Mr. Bonna, these beautiful. Tank you me being here!"

I could hardly hold back the tears. "Kelly, God wouldn't have it any other way, and neither would I. I can't wait to ride beside you tonight. Just don't make me look too bad. You know, maybe I should get someone else to ride with me that won't make me look bad!"

"No, no, no, Mr. Bonna! That not be good. Pete, I, good friends."

I smiled at her. "Kelly, do you know how special you are? Thank you for being you. I love you!" I gave her a big hug.

Kelly and I got the geldings and ourselves all dressed up and sat at the end of the driveway greeting the kids as they came. Pete and Joe stood as stoic as can be as the cars went by.

I looked over at Kelly with her big smile plastered on her face. "Kelly." She looked my way. "Don't you know soldiers aren't suppose to smile at the enemy?"

"But, Mr. Bonna, I never so happy. I pretty."

I had to smile back. "Yes Kelly, you're beautiful."

Kelly and I rode up to the yard just as the sun was setting. We had next to no wind and the moon was as bright as ever. I explained the rules of our game to everyone. We had several questions from kids. I warned them of not spooking the horses and explained where the hot fence was. Judy and Mr. Olson were in charge of the jail where the kids would stay for ten minutes if caught by Kelly or me.

"Okay guys, spread out and start the game. Kelly and I will give you ten minutes to hide before we hunt you down." The kids went in all directions, full of excitement, hoping to never get caught.

I looked over at Kelly as she sat on Pete, proud as a peacock. "Well partner, are you ready to catch some Christians?"

"Yup, Mr. Bonna."

Kelly and I headed west first along the fence line. The little bounce of the saddle seemed to hurt my lower back area. I wondered what that was about? Kelly was on the lookout for our first prisoners. She soon spotted three girls hiding behind a pine tree. We both trotted up to them and drew our swords.

Kelly was all excited. "Stop you! What you doing, you headed to church?"

"We are looking for firewood," they answered back.

Kelly looked at me for direction. "Well Kelly, looking for firewood is not against the law. We'll have to let them go. You kids make sure we don't see you going toward any churches."

We rode south and saw a cardboard church ahead. We trotted Pete and Joe up there and found two kids inside and three behind the box. "Soldier Kelly, looks like we have our first prisoners."

"Yes soldga Bonna, take them to barn. I mean jail."

"Soldier Kelly, you lead the way while I bring up the rear."

"Ya, ya!" Kelly turned Pete northeast and rode ahead like she owned the world. I had to sit back and enjoy the scene. Pete trotted with his necked arched into the bit as Kelly spun and checked the prisoners every once in awhile. She would give the kids commands to stay in a straight line and keep up the pace.

We were coming up to the jail with this first group and Kelly was really taking charge. "Soldga Judy, we brought prisoners, five. Lock them up jail, bad Christians."

Judy looked my way with a slight smile on her face. "Okay, soldier Kelly. Is there anything else?"

Kelly looked my way then back to Judy. "Soldier Judy, have each prisoner do ten pushups before you release them."

Kelly and I prodded them into the barn with our wooden swords. We turned and headed out right away for our next group of prisoners. Kelly soon sniffed out the next group of bad guys and had them heading to jail. As Kelly led, I prompted one kid to try an escape. He took off running through the meadow right when Kelly was doing a spin check. She took a quick glance at me and off she went! Pete responded to her every command. They barreled down on that kid and cut him off at the pass. The rest of the prisoners actually started clapping. They really liked Kelly. Kelly brought that kid back with the point of her sword while Pete did the slow exaggerated trot. Pete was enjoying this as much as Kelly.

During the night we had caught all the kids at least once, except for three guys. I came to find out they would hide up in trees as we passed. They had slips of paper from every cardboard church. We called all the kids in for the next round of "Night of Martyrs." As we had hot apple cider and donuts, the kids were all telling of how they got caught or hid from us. I had to laugh at how many kids got zapped by the hot fence. It seemed like that was a rite of passage for some. Wow! You should have heard the complaints about the pushups.

Pastor Wolbeck from my church came out for the next session. When he started talking, a couple of the adult leaders, along with Mr. Olson and myself headed toward the fire scene. We could hear Pastor Wolbeck explain to the kids what was next as we got ready. "This is called 'Night of Martyrs' because back in the day most of you would have been thrown in jail and then burned on a cross for not denouncing Jesus. If you look behind, you will see three people hanging on crosses."

The kids turned around to see three people hanging on crosses about one hundred yards away. The fire was between the kids and the prisoners.

I stood off to the side a little and shouted, "This is your last chance to denounce Jesus! Save yourself and denounce Him and you will live!"

The three prisoners called out to their Jesus and ignored my pleas.

"You will now burn where you hang!" I lit the fire. The kids couldn't tell from that distance that the fire was actually twenty yards away from the prisoners. The fire raged within minutes with the lighter fluid we had sprayed on it. The three prisoners were soon screaming in fake pain, pretending they were getting consumed by the fire. Wow, the one lady had the eeriest scream I ever heard. It gave me goose bumps.

Another leader and I were shouting insults at them as they burned on the cross where they hung. Eventually, the three prisoners snuck down off their crosses and hid after replacing their crosses with half burned crosses we had ready. I quietly walked back by the kids and listened to Pastor Wolbecks' closing words.

"Guys, look out there. You now see three empty partially burned crosses. Jesus hung on a similar cross for you and I. The only way to be with Jesus is to verbally ask Him into your heart. You can't be nice enough, you can't be good enough, you can't have your own plan to get to heaven." He turned and quietly looked at the fire.

Pastor Wolbeck turned back to the kids. "How do you guys like the 'Night of Martyrs'?"

The kids were all excited about the fire, Pete, Joe and spending time in jail. They again talked of having to do push-ups and running into the hot fence.

I closed the evening with a prayer and thanked all the kids for coming out. "If any of you have any questions, please talk with any of the adults helping here tonight. Goodnight."

I headed back towards the fire to check on it, and a heavy set boy who was visiting approached me as we walked. "Pastor, I'm confused. My dad says Jesus was just a nice guy that had great karma." He seemed nervous to even say this.

"Hi, my name is Jude." I held out my hand to shake his.

"My name is Steve."

"Well Steve, who do you think Jesus is?" I asked.

He looked down and kicked at the ground. "I just don't know who he really is, Pastor."

"That's fine Steve, most of us have been in the same place at one time. I always look to the Bible, God's book of truth for answers on who Jesus is."

"Really?" Steve sounded surprised.

We sat down on a hay bale and I said a quick silent prayer for God's guidance before I started. "Jesus is so awesome! He is God's own Son, sent down to earth in human flesh and worked as a carpenter. Jesus is perfect in every way. That means he never sinned. Jesus loves you and I so much that he took a beating and then hung on a cross till dead for yours and my sins." I reached out and touched Steve on his shoulder. "Three days later he rose from the dead and to this day is the only God to be resurrected. Think about it Steve, how many other two thousand year old carpenters have their birthday celebrated every year?" I stopped and looked at Steve.

Steve sat there shaking his head. "Pastor, even if that is all true, what's that got to do with me getting to heaven?"

"Jesus answered that in the book of John with his own words in verse 3:3 'I tell you the truth, no one can see the kingdom of God unless he is born again.' Jesus loves you more than you can imagine, and he wants to spend eternity with you. A person needs to ask Jesus into their hearts and repent of sins. That's how Jesus allows man into heaven."

I'm not sure what to think, that seems so strange to me right now. Can I think about that and maybe we talk again someday?"

"Why certainly, let's trade phone numbers. I'll call you in

the next couple days. Maybe we can get some ice cream or something." Steve thanked me and headed to his car.

After everyone left, Kelly and I went to put Pete and Joe into the pasture. It seemed Joe had a little limp in the left front when I led him out of the barn. What was going on there? Kelly scooted home and I went into the house, exhausted.

I had very full weeks of horses lined up for trimming now that it was spring. Many people don't trim their horses when it is the dead of winter. I would leave before sunup and not get home till after dark. Judy worked the afternoon shifts, so Pete and Joe were kind of on their own. I came home one night late and Pete was the only one waiting for me at the hay feeder. I went into the house to get a flashlight. As I walked back out I whistled for Joe. I thought I heard him answer back.

I jumped up on Pete. "Pete, take me to Joe, big guy."

Pete turned and we rode off in the darkness. Pete whinnied a couple times as we walked. Joe would answer back. That was a good sign. Pete walked right up to Joe as he stood by an Ironwood tree. I jumped down with my flashlight to see what was going on.

"Hey Joe, what's wrong?" He stood there with his left front foot extended out with very little weight on it. I reminded myself that he had limped after the Night of Martyrs. I looked for blood and cuts on his leg. I slipped his rope halter on and tried to see if he would walk. Wow! He could barely walk. I gradually led him up to the barn and into the lighted area. You could see the pain in his eyes.

"Okay Joe, I'm going to lift that foot and see if you have a nail in it or something." I grabbed my hoof jack, hoof pick, and an extra quartz light. I cleaned the bottom of his foot with a wire brush and shown the light on it. There weren't any nails or screws, so I started squeezing on his sole with my hoof pliers. Oh boy, he sure let me know when I hit the sore spot. He immediately pulled his foot away.

"Joe, looks like we have ourselves an abscess." I probed some more with the hoof pliers to try to find the core of it. Joe was getting impatient with the whole process. "Joe, I know this hurts, but stick with me. I'm sorry I didn't check on you sooner, big guy."

I went to the house and got hot soapy water in one bucket and hot Epsom salts in another bucket. I started scrubbing his foot clean so I could cut in and find that abscess. With a black marker I outlined where I thought the abscess was. My hoof knife was good and sharp, so I started carving away sole in the center of my outline. Carving on the sole doesn't hurt them at all, it's the stuff under the sole that gets a horse's attention. Joe's sole was good and thick. I slowed down the deeper I got.

Pop! The abscess blew up as soon as I took the last layer of sole away. Yuck, it was under pressure and blew crap all over. Let me tell you, that stuff had the worst smell of rotten flesh. I had found the geyser. I dug out a little bigger hole so it could drain well. After the crap was done coming out, it started bleeding. That was good; bleeding means it is cleaning itself from the inside.

I grabbed a curry comb and soft brush and placed Joe's foot in the Epsom salts solution. "Joe, old buddy, we need to soak that foot for at least twenty minutes. How about I brush you while I wait?"

Time seems to slow to a crawl when soaking a foot. Joe stood there like a trooper while I brushed him. Pete stood outside and whinnied every once in awhile, wondering what was going on.

As I looked into his eyes I said, "Joe, this whole deal is a long process. You're going to have to be a good patient. Ya know, it seems like I'm in the same boat at times. I get this awful taste in my mouth and then nagging pains in my guts. What do you think that is, Joe?" He nudged me with his head. "Believe it or not, I wonder if Judy's cooking has anything to do with it. Maybe we're both getting old, Joe. Ya think?" He nickered at me and rubbed his head against my chest.

My next step was to mix up a poultice of sugar and iodine into a paste and pack it into the hole I had dug. "Easy Joe, foot." I smeared the paste into the hole and wrapped his foot with some cardboard and duct tape. I asked God to heal Joe and then headed into the house.

I got up at five the next morning to check on Joe. Yep, his foot wrapping was all gone. I brought him up to the barn and cleaned out the hole I had dug the day before. Digging with the hoof pick was tedious work. Joe would let me know right now if I was too deep. The last little dirt I flushed out with a syringe. I smelled the open hole in his sole. Yuck, it still reeked. I dug more sole away hoping to get more drainage. It was pretty ugly. His inner foot looked like hamburger. More time in Epsom salts. While he soaked, I did my devotions for the day.

Proverbs 20:29: "The glory of young men is their strength, gray hair the splendor of the old." That was my Bible verse for devotions that morning. What was God telling me? I sat there in silence; God had given me my fair share of strength. That seemed to make sense at my age. I hated to think about it, but when I didn't feel good, I actually felt like an old man. "God, either I'm not understanding you this morning or I'm not listening well, one of the two. Lord, I have plans to be young for a long time. If you're talking to me about being old, well that just doesn't seem right." I finished with the Lord's prayer.

I stood up and talked with Joe. "Joe, what do you think. Are we going to grow old together? I hate to say it buddy, but man lives longer than horses." I looked him in the eyes. "I can't imagine having to say goodbye to you and Pete someday. What will I do without you two nags?" All of a sudden, Joe got real nervous and started snorting. "Joe, I'm sorry! I guess I don't mean to sound so glum in front of you. We have many years together, big guy."

It took at least one month of working with Joe's foot twice daily: soaking, wrapping, praying, repeating. Each time I picked it up I smelled it. It took three weeks before the smell totally went away. It was a good day when I finally felt I could just let Joe heal the rest of the way on his own.

Chapter 14
"God Closes a Door"

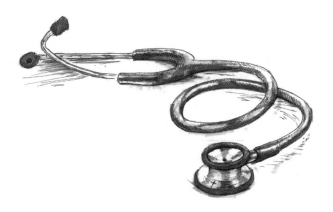

Life was moving on. Becky and Wade were raising and selling hitch horses. Wade was doing fine with the farm life and Mom and Dad were enjoying their grandkids being so close. Judy and I were busy with our own lives in Paynesville. My trimming business was going very well and Judy was excelling at her job.

Many mornings I'd wake up with that awful taste in my mouth. Judy would complain of my breath smelling bad.

"Jude, you need to get checked by a doctor to see what's going on."

"Oh, honey, I'll be all right. It's just an upset stomach or something."

In reality, I was consistently feeling bad. I was just trying to be tough. Trimming horses was getting harder and harder. It just seemed I was losing my strength. Then, one day while trimming, I again had to step behind the barn and puke several times. My gut was tied up in knots after that episode. I had less and less of an appetite and I was starting to wonder what was next.

As always, God was there to lead me. I was at church one day getting ready for youth group when our head minister approached me. "Hey, Jude, how are you doing?"

"Oh, just fine, Pastor Wolbeck, just getting ready for youth group," I answered.

He handed me his Bible. "Could you look up Exodus 20:16 please and read it to me?"

"Sure." As I started to page toward Exodus I said, "Isn't that part of the Ten Commandments?"

"Just read it, please," he said abruptly.

"Okay, Exodus 20:16: 'Thou shall not give false testimony.'

"What does that mean, Jude?"

"Well, it's pretty simple, tell no lies, Pastor Wolbeck."

"Yes! Now, I'll repeat my question. How are you doing, Jude?" He looked me straight in the eyes. "I'm not blind, Jude. If I didn't know you better, I'd say you were doing meth or something. Have you gone in for a checkup?"

I was shocked that Pastor Wolbeck sensed something wrong with me. "Oh, I just have some bug in my stomach or something. It will pass in a few weeks."

"Jude, now you are giving false testimony to yourself. The sad part is you believe it. Now you get to a doctor and get on the mend or we'll have to let you go as youth pastor. You can't lead our youth if you are not honest with yourself." As he walked away my first reaction was to get mad, but I knew he was right. The next day I called the doctor and set up an appointment for a physical.

Two weeks later I was sitting in the doctor's office in Sauk Centre, Minnesota. She checked the normal things, like blood pressure, heart rate, breathing, and reflexes. I have to admit it was not the most fun standing there in my whitie tighties while a woman doctor probed every part of my body. Next thing I knew, I was heading down to the lab in one of those hospital gowns. If that doesn't humble a man, nothing will. After the lab work, I was able to go back to her exam room to put my clothes back on.

Soon there was a knock on the door. "Yes, sir." I answered as Dr. Joyce Brand stepped into the exam room. "Oh, sorry ma'am," I sheepishly apologized.

"Jude, how long have you been feeling this way?" she asked.

"I suppose it's been three to four months since I first noticed it."

"Has it always been this bad, or has it gotten worse?"

"Many days I feel pretty good. Other days I feel pretty bad. It comes and goes. Lately it seems to be getting worse."

She checked her clip board and wrote a few more things down, and then closely checked my eyes again. "We need to get the results back from your lab work before we can make any suggestions. I want you to schedule another appointment with the receptionist for Thursday before you leave."

I blurted out, "I'm not sure that is necessary, Dr. Brand."

"Jude, you don't have a choice." She looked directly at me. "This has me pretty concerned. You might consider bringing Judy along so we can talk."

"Wow, bummer," I said to myself as I walked out of the exam room. I set up the next appointment and went to my car. I sat there trying to collect myself and talk with God. "God, you know what you have in store for me. May I always praise you and glorify your name. Amen."

On the way home I stopped and ordered some Chinese carryout for supper. Judy was feeding Pete and Joe when I got home. She pretty much had them spoiled by now. She was brushing them as they ate hay.

"How is the prettiest woman in the world doing?" I said as I walked up to the fence.

She came over and gave me a kiss and a hug. "Never mind me, what did the doctor say today?"

"She said it was a common ailment among young married men. Yes, ma'am, only she's never seen it quite this bad before." I gazed into Judy's eyes. "It all comes down to too much housework, dishes, sweeping, you know the sort." I burst out laughing. "Now I bought us some carryout Chinese, so let's go eat before it gets cold."

Judy and I ate dinner, then headed back to the barn so we could talk about the doctor visit while spending time with Pete and Joe. We sat there in the feed bunk as Pete and Joe chewed on hay. "Judy, the doctor wants me back on Thursday so we can discuss the results of the lab work. She also mentioned that you might want to come."

Judy looked my way to see if I was kidding. "What do you mean, Jude? Is that all she said?"

"The only other thing that was said besides the normal check up was a few questions on how long I've felt this way and stuff like that. At the end she did say she was concerned."

Judy placed her head into her hands and just sat there in silence for the longest time. I figured it was best to let her be and let her absorb what was said. She looked away from me as she rubbed her eyes. "Jude Bonner, I love you! And yes, I'll be with you for that next appointment."

I walked up to her back and put my arms around her and

just held her. "Everything will be all right, why certainly, why certainly. How 'bout we saddle up the geldings and go for a ride?"

It was a beautiful night for a ride. The frogs were singing, the pheasants were cackling, and Pete and Joe were true gentlemen. We rode for over an hour and then headed to the house. I was pretty tired by then, so we said our prayers and I went to bed.

As we drove to the doctor's appointment, Judy told me she had put me on the prayer chain at church. I don't really know why, but I had a hard time with that. I guess a person thinks that the prayer chain is only for others who are really sick. I wasn't mad at Judy for what she did, but I really didn't think it was needed.

Dr. Brand probed around at my gut some, looked into my eyes with that light thing, and then sat down. "Jude, have you felt any better since our last visit?"

"Maybe a little."

"Good. Okay, now we need to run some more tests to get to the bottom of this. Our lab work seems to be pointing towards the liver, so I've scheduled a DCP and AFP test for first thing tomorrow morning at the St. Cloud Hospital. Those tests will check your liver function to make sure it is doing its job. Jude, you will need to fast until after those tests are complete. It will probably take about two hours of your time and you'll need someone to drive you home."

Judy and I looked at each other in silence. I thought to myself I was glad Judy had put us on the prayer chain.

"Dr. Brand, what do you think this is all about?" I asked.

"It seems to be the liver, Jude. The tests in St. Cloud will tell us if arteries feeding the liver are restricted or if there might be a cancer."

Judy stood up immediately and walked over to the window. Dr. Brand continued, "The results from the DCP and AFP will be ready this weekend. You will need to be in St. Cloud Monday morning to meet with them to go over the results."

Judy said with a shaky voice, "Tell us what is next."

"It's best to wait, Judy. We can speculate and come up with many what-ifs or maybes. The thing I can do is hand Jude off to the experts at St. Cloud and let them do their jobs."

As I gritted my teeth, I thanked Dr. Brand for all her help. I started to put my shirt back on as Judy stared out the window. The room was dead silent until I started softly singing, "It is well, with my soul." I needed to do that to stay strong in the Lord.

After one verse of the song, Dr. Brand stated, "Judy, Jude, I see you really believe in a god." She shook her head slightly. "Have you ever thought of yoga or meditation?"

I stopped with my buttons and looked her straight in the eyes. "That's of the devil, Dr. Brand. Don't ever push your new age crap on me again. Jeremiah 30 – But I will restore you to health and heal your wounds, declares the Lord."

"Jude, I'm only trying to help you as your doctor."

I didn't even bother looking at her again. "Our Father who art in Heaven, Hallowed be thy name…"

She quickly left the room with her nose in the air.

Afterward, we quietly left her office and headed home. I was pretty mad. Judy sent an update to the prayer chain and soon the phone was ringing. Judy was having a hard time, so I did all the talking. I was doing pretty well until I heard Mom's voice at the other end. "Jude?"

"Yes, Mom?"

"How you doing, son?" she asked with a quiver in her voice.

"I feel great right now. Dr. Brand is pretty concerned, so we have more tests in St. Cloud tomorrow morning."

Mom was silent for a while. "What can I do to help? Do I need to go with you in the morning?"

"Thank you, Mom, but I think this is something Judy and I need to do together."

"You let me know if I need to bring food over or clean the house, whatever."

"Mom, we'll be fine. I'm sure Dr. Brand is just covering all the possibilities. Monday we go back for the results. I think the tests will just show some stomach bug or something. Come to think of it, you can always bring over one of them pecan pies of yours."

"Jude Bonner, if you're thinking of pie you can't be that sick. Now get your butt to bed and get a good night's sleep. Dad and I will be praying for you."

Judy and I went to bed and I just held her for the longest time. We said a few prayers and slept well until first light. We did chores, cleaned up, and then headed off to St. Cloud in the rain. Judy brought her Bible and read verses as I drove. Dr. Brand was right. After the tests, the last thing I wanted to do was drive home.

It was a long, grueling weekend waiting for Monday's results. I had a hard time focusing on my duties. I played over in my mind one hundred different ideas of what the test results would show. It was a bright sunny day as Judy and I drove to St. Cloud. Not much was said during that thirty-minute drive.

Judy and I sat in the waiting room as quiet as church mice. I was looking at a few magazines when I heard, "Jude Bonner, you can come in now."

I looked at Judy and she clasped my hand. That thirty-foot walk into the examination room seemed like thirty miles. The nurse took my blood pressure and other vitals and stepped out of the room.

It wasn't long and Dr. Baki stepped into the room. He was a dark complexioned man that only stood five-foot-two inches. We said our hello's and he proceeded to do a little examination of my middle torso. He poked pretty deep and I felt some pain in certain areas. When I cringed, he would look at me with concern in his big dark brown eyes. The room was silent.

"Mr. Bonner, how old are you?" he asked.

"Twenty-nine."

"Have you been feeling any different?"

"I think so. Yes, a little."

"Well, Mr. Bonner, we have the test results back and I'm sorry to say they aren't real good."

Judy walked over and stood beside me, grabbing for my hand. She was trembling with emotion. "Mr. Bonner, the tests show you have an early stage of cancer attacking the liver." I could feel a lump in my throat the size of a volleyball as he continued. "You need to make some decisions soon. First, are you going to get a second opinion and second, if our tests are correct, are you willing to do chemo and radiation?" He scribbled on his clip board. "Now is the time for you to ask me any questions."

Judy squeezed my hand as hard as she could as we sat there in silence. I looked at Judy and she stared at the wall fighting back tears. Dr. Baki handed her a box of tissues. Dr. Baki asked, "May I say a few things that will hopefully help you on this journey?" I nodded in agreement. "This is going to test you like you have never been tested. The good news is we have caught it fairly early and you are a strong young man. The bad news is that the tests show this is an aggressive type of cancer. The liver is a vital organ and cancer of the liver is a very serious illness."

"Doc, how long do I have?" I asked.

Dr. Baki paused as he rubbed his brow. "One to five years I

would say. It depends on how you respond to treatment, your attitude, and your faith."

"Dr. Baki, Judy and I will need some time to grab hold of this one. We'll get back to you with our questions. I want to thank you for your time this morning."

Dr. Baki nodded and left the office. Judy was biting her lip trying to stop from crying. I stood up from the exam table and held her. As I wrapped my arms around her she literally collapsed as I held her up.

As Judy sobbed, I whispered into her ear, "Romans 8:28: 'And we know that in all things God works for the good of those who love him, who have been called according to his purpose.'"

Judy pushed herself away from me and snapped back, "Well, excuse me, Jude Bonner, but I just don't get God's plan right this very moment!"

"Judy, you heard Dr. Baki say that this was going to be a test like we've never seen before. Now please, I need to fight this and most of that fight will be fought with God at my side. So look me in the eye and please listen." As I grabbed her hands, we stood face to face. "You need to help me fight this, and Jude Bonner is not going let some cancer thing separate me from God's plan. Now are we in agreement that you will stand by me and God and work through this?"

"Why, Jude, why us?" Judy was nearly hysterical.

"Okay, honey, please settle down. Will you say the Lord's prayer with me right now?"

Judy stood there in dead silence. I don't think she even heard my request. We stood there holding hands as I recited the Lord's prayer. I felt a calm come over me as I finished with an "Amen. We have to go now, honey."

I took Judy's hand and headed to the door. When we got outside, Judy lost it again. She fell against me sobbing as we struggled to get to the car.

Chapter 15
"The Battle"

Judy and I did get a second opinion and it showed the same results. After that, we decided to tell our families, close friends, and our youth group. Wow! Telling the kids in youth group was a very hard thing to do. I felt like I was letting them down. I even saw a few tears from the guys as I told them my story. The kids had the normal questions for us and asked what they could do to help. Then they all gathered around Judy and me and prayed over us. That was pretty rough to take for this Minnesota German boy.

I said to the guys in the youth group, "You know, guys, there will be times that I will be very weak from the treatments. So you might catch a time that a few of you might be able to take me. But don't get your hopes up too high and remember to pack a lunch!" With that I attacked a couple of the guys closest to me.

Judy and I tried our best to keep life as normal as possible at this stage of the battle. It got hard to do when everyone was dropping off food and cards in the mail all the time. I was actually feeling pretty good since the diagnosis. I was back to trimming feet full time and Judy seemed to be holding her own too.

The radiation and chemo started and was a pain, not only physically, but in the time it took. Judy or Mom would drive me to St. Cloud for the treatments. My body seemed to be handling the onslaught of the treatments fairly well, except for my hair. Fourteen days after my first treatment, my hair started coming out in globs. Soon Jude was bald as a cue ball! I would come home from the treatments pretty worn out. I would usually go out to the pasture and sit with Pete and Joe and we'd talk. Maybe I'm crazy, but they seemed to understand what I was going through. I would lay on their backs and rub their necks.

Harold and Perry came over with their families one evening to see us. Each was married now and had kids. It was great to see them since we had really lost track of each other after high school. As always, I think it was hard for Judy to see the little kids when we were still childless. Harold and Perry were doing well. They each had good jobs and a strong faith in Jesus Christ. After they left, Judy found an envelope containing three hundred dollars and a note from the guys. Judy wept.

Dad called me and asked if he and Mom could come over after church one Sunday. Judy and I got the house all cleaned up before they came. Mom insisted on bringing lunch over. After lunch Dad asked, "Jude, do you feel up to going for a ride with me on the geldings?"

Well, it didn't take much persuading for me to go ride horses! Soon Dad and I had the geldings saddled up and heading down the trail. It was a beautiful day.

"Jude, how are you doing?"

"Oh, I'm fine, Dad."

"How is the money working out for you so far?"

"That is going okay so far. Insurance is covering everything at this time. Not sure what the future will bring financially. Praise God that Judy has a very good job."

"Just checking. Son, are you updated on a will and life insurance, stuff like that?"

"Yes, we have met with a financial planner guy from church and we are sitting okay right now."

"Do your mother and I need to get you any money to help out?"

"Thanks, Dad, but no thanks. This is something Judy, God and I need to do on our own right now."

"Your mother and I are praying for you every day, son, and I know many others are doing the same. You need to promise me one thing, Jude."

"What's that, Dad?"

"That you will call your mother and me if there is anything we can do to help. Chores, lawn mowing, whatever you need."

"Why certainly, why certainly!" I laughed.

Dad and I rode six miles that afternoon. Pete and Joe were pretty tired when we came home. Mom was upset as we pulled in the yard, thinking I was overdoing it by riding that long. I started to dread the treatments every three weeks. I would just start feeling halfway normal and then I'd have to drive to St. Cloud to get kicked in the teeth again. As the treatments went on, the more tired and worn out I became. I had lost twenty pounds by now, since food just didn't appeal to me during the treatments. I soon had to end my trimming business because I had no energy or strength left in me. Judy and I sat down and wrote out postcards to each of my clients explaining what had to be done. It was kind of neat because a few of them continued to pay me every five weeks like I was still trimming their horses' hooves.

I will never forget the day Judy and I were driving to St. Cloud for my last treatment. I was pretty chipper that day. "Mrs. Bonner, how much you want to bet that after treatment today I'll feel good enough to buy a chocolate milkshake on the way home?"

"Now, that's a pretty heavy proposition, Mr. Bonner. I'd say ten back rubs is what I'm willing to bet." She laughed.

"You got it! Just wait and see, Mrs. Bonner, I'm gonna hold you to it. Them back rubs will feel awful nice."

Let me tell you, when I came out of that treatment the last thing I wanted was a chocolate milkshake. But I couldn't forget about the bet. As we passed the burger place, I had Judy pull in.

"Jude, are you serious? Do you want me to go through the drive-thru?"

"Nope, just pull into that parking spot over there. I need to walk in and get my milkshake. Would you like one, honey?"

What Judy didn't realize was I had no intention of eating this milkshake. I would take it home and save it till I felt better. I dragged myself out of the car and headed in the side door. I was very weak and the smell of food when I stepped in, almost overtook me. As I staggered over to the counter to place my order, I was getting stares from several of the workers.

"May I help you?" asked the young lady behind the counter.

"Ma'am, today is a special day for me and I'd like a large chocolate milkshake. Is that something you can do for me?"

"Yes, sir. Is there anything else I can get for you?"

I almost asked her for a new liver, but luckily I caught myself. Asking for a new liver was only a way for me to get pity. I reminded myself that God would not be honored by me seeking pity.

"No, ma'am, that is all I need right now."

"That will be $3.85, sir."

"Here is a five, and please do me the favor of keeping the change on my special day."

"Why, thank you, sir, and may I ask why this is your special day?"

"Today I placed a bet for ten back rubs with my lovely young bride that I would buy a chocolate milkshake after my last treatment. Now she is waiting for me in the car, so if you can excuse me, ma'am."

"Thank you, sir."

"Ma'am, I thank you and may God bless you."

I made my way to the car which seemed like a four mile walk. Judy was knitting as she waited. I put the milkshake in the door box and sat down.

"Yes, ma'am, those back rubs are going to feel pretty good. I do believe it was ten that we agreed upon. Is that right, honey?"

"Okay, mister, but first you have to eat that thing as I drive home!"

"Now honey, if you will remember, the bet was that I would buy a milkshake after treatment and I just bought one. I never said anything about eating it. Now let's hurry home, miss, before it starts to melt." I laughed.

"Jude Bonner! That wasn't fair!"

"How many times have I told you, God never promised life to be fair!"

I slept most of the way home as Judy drove. The milkshake made it home also and was put in the freezer for a later day.

Our next trip back to St. Cloud for doctoring was scheduled for two months from my last treatment.

Chapter 16
"Winning or Losing the Battle"

After the last treatment it took me about three weeks before I started feeling okay. I was getting my appetite back and feeling a little stronger each day. I even trimmed one foot a day on Pete and Joe. I was also doing some basic exercises to help get some muscle tone back, and eventually I started trimming a few horses a day and was feeling pretty good. My hair was starting to grow back and it was curly. People didn't recognize me with hair, especially curly hair.

I was given the go-ahead to head up the youth pastor role at church again by the elder board. It felt great to worship our God with the youth group again. Life was returning to the way it had been before my illness. Judy was sleeping better and seemed to be going strong with her job. I even had the strength to wrestle with Becky's kids and play all the important games like hide and seek, tag, and kickball.

Judy and I went on a cruise that spring as a celebration for getting through the treatments. It was only a five-day cruise, but I must admit, it was very nice. The dancing, food, pools, and late-night shows were pretty cool. When we got off the boat in Florida, it was seventy-five degrees. When we got off the plane in the Twin Cities, it was twenty-four below zero. That was a one-hundred-degree swing!

Soon, Judy and I were heading back to St. Cloud for my two month check-up. "Honey, are you ready to make that milkshake bet again?"

"How can you think of milkshakes on a day like this? Aren't you worried what the doctor will say?"

"It's a guy thing, honey. Guys are just wired differently. That's why God made male and female."

"How 'bout that wired guy says a prayer as we go?"

"Sure, honey. It's going to be fine."

Judy and I prayed and thanked God the rest of the way and even sang a few worship songs. Before we knew it, we were in Dr. Baki's waiting room. As the nurse brought us to a room, she took my height and weight. Both of those numbers looked good. The nurse took my vitals in the room and left.

Judy reminisced, "It seems like just yesterday that we stood here waiting to meet this cancer specialist. I don't think I will ever forget that day."

Dr. Baki knocked on the door and then stepped in. "Jude, Judy, how have you been?"

"Pretty good, pretty good," I answered.

Dr. Baki asked about my appetite, strength, pain, and the taste in my mouth. He even asked about our love life. "Okay, I've asked enough questions. Let me listen to you breathe and probe around to see what I find. We will also send you down to lab for a urine sample and blood tests." Dr. Baki checked my gums, my eyes, and the color of my finger and toenails. He pinched my skin to see how long it would stand up, and he probed around my gut forever. He would write a few things on his chart and come back to pry and probe some more.

"Okay, folks, you need to get down to lab for those samples. We won't know the results of those tests until early next week. I will call you as soon as I read the results. What I can say at this time is that so far you look and respond well to my checks. If the blood work shows us positive results, then I'd like to see you again in six months. Any questions?"

"No, I guess not," I said and looked at Judy.

Judy and I sat in the waiting room for the lab work. We both noticed a couple of little kids who were there for some type of test. One was in a wheelchair, another was on portable oxygen. I thought, "I guess I don't have it all that bad in the first place."

We were soon on our way home after the lab work. I even talked Judy into a milkshake.

For four days Judy was on pins and needles waiting for the

call. On Monday morning Judy had to work, so I stuck around home to catch the phone. I have to admit it was hard not to run all the scenarios through my mind as I waited for the call. At 10:33 the phone finally rang.

"Hello?"

"Yes, Jude, this is Dr. Baki calling. I have reviewed the test results and have some answers for you. Is Judy able to get on the phone with us?"

I hesitated for a second. "No, she is working today." I thought if he was asking for Judy, then it was not good news.

"Okay then. The tests show your blood counts are pretty good, but not where they should be. The blood tests give us the most information and it is not uncommon for them to be low at this stage. The other tests that we did came back showing signs of healing, so I'm feeling good about those. We will need to see you in another six months and will check your blood counts at that time. In the meantime, you are to go on with your life. Keep taking your medications and be careful not to overdo it until your strength comes back."

"Thank you, Dr. Baki. We really appreciate all that you've done."

"Jude, keep in mind the food charts we sent home with you, and after I see you in six months, I hope to never see you again in my office. Bye."

"Goodbye."

I hung up the phone and praised God immediately. "Jesus, you are so awesome. Thank you for getting me through this! Jesus, I thank you for each day you give me. I need to praise you in the highs and lows, Lord. You are holy and just, Lord. In Christ's name, amen."

It wasn't two minutes after Dr. Baki called that the phone rang again.

"Hello?"

"Jude, have you heard from the doctor yet?" Mom asked.

"Yes, Mom. I just hung up the phone with him. I don't have to go back for six months!"

There was a dead silence at Mom's end of the phone. I heard some sniffles as Mom was trying to regain her composure.

"Thank you, Jesus. Thank you, Lord," Mom cried out. "Okay, would it be all right for Dad and I and Becky's family to take you guys out to dinner tonight? That way Judy can take a break from cooking."

"You know, I think Judy and I would like that. I'll call her and let her know. Goodbye."

I called Judy's work number to see if she was by the desk.

"Paynesville Hospital, this is Judy."

"Hi, honey. How is it going?"

"Jude Bonner, I'll answer as soon as you tell me what Dr. Baki said."

"Promise to kiss me when you get home?"

"Jude, I'm working so cut the romance, please."

"Would you believe we are going out for dinner with Becky, Wade and my parents to celebrate that I don't need to go back for six months?"

There was the longest hesitation on Judy's end. "Oh, Jude, I don't know what to say," she said with a sob in her throat.

"How bout you love me? And Jude Bonner is the greatest husband in the world?"

"Oh, Jude, you know I love you but I'd better get going. Thanks for calling."

Our whole crew celebrated in Sauk Centre that night and had a great time. I was able to sit between two of my nephews. Now, that's a position everyone should be in at one time or another. Conway was older than Oliver, so he thought he needed to tell Oliver what to eat and when. They had more food on the floor than in their tummies. I sat there just thanking the Lord for little kids. They are blessings!

I gradually worked my way back to full time trimming on horses. It was hard to believe how much muscle tone I had lost. Pete and Joe were doing well and Judy and I rode them a lot that fall. That winter was almost perfect for giving sleigh rides as there was just enough snow and it wasn't too cold. Christmas time was the busiest time. There were days Pete and Joe were out five and six times a day. They were in pretty good shape after that. Our best passengers were a group of mentally handicapped adults. Dad came over and helped get the people up on the rack. Those people were so happy and appreciative, and it was such a privilege to see them smile. That ride we did for free.

Before we knew it, Judy and I were heading back for my six month check-up. They did the same old stuff: poking, probing, blood work, and sending us home with a promise to call with results later.

As I drove home, Judy started crying. "Hey, honey, what's up?"

"The way Dr. Baki acted today has me scared, Jude," she said, wiping away tears. "His facial expressions and tone of voice were different than before. Didn't you notice?"

"Oh, honey you're reading way too much into it. I feel fine! Ya know, we're only a mile away from the milkshakes."

Women's intuition is many times right. We got a call from Dr. Baki asking us to come in and meet with him the next day. We were pretty quiet as we drove to St. Cloud. Dr. Baki explained the cancer was back in my liver and that I had spots on my spleen and kidneys. He was straightforward when I asked what the future would bring.

"Jude, you are a very sick young man inside, and soon you will start to feel it. I just wish I could fix you. What I see is a fast-growing cancer that will give you maybe a year."

Judy and I sat there expressionless. My mind was trying to grasp what was just said. Was I dreaming? Did Dr. Baki call in the wrong patient? Did he look at the test results incorrectly? My mind was in big-time denial. This could not be happening to me. Judy and I were going to live happily ever after.

The silence was broken by Dr. Baki. "In the meantime, continue life as is. You and Judy might want to travel while you still feel up to it. You will eventually need pain medications and maybe a change in your dietary needs. Barring a miracle, you will start getting weaker and losing your stamina. Please call me with any questions twenty-four-seven. My cell number is on my card. I wish I could do more, Jude."

Dr. Baki quietly left the room. As I sat there, the anger started to build up inside of me. Why me? What did I do wrong? This is supposed to happen to someone else! Yes, sir, I was having an old-fashioned pity party. As I sat there creating my own misery, Judy quietly slipped out of the room. That just added to my misery! I said to myself that she must not even care. Soon she was back and asked me to come with her to see someone.

I thought we were going to see another doctor. We took the elevator down to the pediatric floor. The nurse brought us to a window and we looked in and saw a little girl reading a book with her mom. The nurse told us her name was Susan. She was four years old and she had an inoperable tumor on the brain.

Right then God spoke to me. "Go in and talk with her."

I asked the nurse if I could go in to say "hello." "Yes, you may," she answered.

As I stepped into the room, little Susan looked my way with her big brown eyes and smiled at me. "Hi, my name is Susan. What's your name?"

"Jude."

"Do you have an owie like I do?"

"I'm not sure, Susan."

"Mommy, can Mr. Jude read me a story?"

"Why, sure he can, if he wishes," Susan's mother said.

God has a plan for each of us and that moment was a God moment. I sat there with that little blond-haired girl in my arms reading Humpty Dumpty Sat on the Wall.

When I was done she said, "Mommy says my owie is kind of like Humpty Dumpty. We're not sure if I can be put back together again." She gazed into my eyes.

I hugged her and kissed her little blond head as I held her in my arms.

"Mommy says Jesus will take care of me. Do you know Jesus, Mr. Jude?"

"Yes, Susan, I surely do," I answered as I fought back tears.

"Why are you crying, Mr. Jude? Big people don't cry."

I held her even tighter and gave her another kiss on her forehead as my eyes flooded with tears. God allowed me to hold Susan, one of his precious children that day as He spoke with me.

"Jude," God said, "It'll be okay. Trust in me."

As I continued to hold Susan, God's hand came over me and all my fears left me immediately. I silently praised God for what he had given me.

"Mr. Jude, would you pray with me?"

"Yes."

Susan and I prayed to the Almighty Father in heaven that afternoon. How precious to hear a little four-year-old pray from her heart to our Heavenly Father.

"Susan, can I come back and visit you another day?"

"Mommy, can Mr. Jude come back and visit us at our home someday?" Susan asked her mom.

"Yes, honey, he is welcome anytime."

Judy and Susan's mom exchanged phone numbers while Susan and I played ring around the rosie. We said our goodbyes and Judy and I headed for home.

All I could think about on the way home was visiting sick kids in the hospital. I talked to Judy about it and she helped me set up a plan of action as we drove. Judy was driving and I was writing everything down. God is good!

Chapter 17
"A New Treatment"

Judy and I decided not to tell everyone what Dr. Baki had said. We decided that when they asked us how things were going, we would just ask them to pray for healing. Judy was strong but she had a hard time being strong when she faced Mom the first time. Judy cried a lot in Mom's arms, and Mom looked at me with a stoic look in her eye as she held Judy. Mom knew what the truth was without anyone telling her.

Of course I wasn't much better when Dad asked me in the barn. I tried everything to not look him in the eye. It's kind of funny that I thought Dad wouldn't see right through me!

"Jude, how long?"

"Maybe a year or less is what he guessed." I stood there trying to be strong. "Can I ask a favor?"

"Sure."

"I'd appreciate it if you would make a casket for me." Dad stood there silently putting the squeeze on a pitch fork handle and looking off in the distance. "If you feel up to it, we could hitch the geldings and snake a few Ash logs to have sawn into boards. That would be very special to me," I said.

He grabbed his handkerchief and wiped his eyes. "Your ma and I will miss you more than you can ever imagine. Why, I remember holding you for the first time just after you were born. I remember you catching your first toad. I remember your first stitches, the first time you drove the old 'H.'" He flipped some hay with his pitchfork. "I remember telling you about the birds and the bees. I remember whooping on you as we wrestled." He laughed softly. "I remember your first broken heart when Tammy Novak already had a date for the eighth grade homecoming dance. I remember the trials you went through to break them geldings. I remember the afternoon when Judy came to Christ," Dad stammered as he tried to keep his composure. "I remember your wedding day as you stood there proud as can be, and rightfully so! And now you're telling me I have to bury you. My God, Jesus why?" Dad whispered as he stabbed his fork into a bale of straw.

I stood there in silence. What could I say? I'd never seen Dad in so much pain before. I quietly left and did calf chores while Dad regained his composure. Then I returned to the barn. "Dad, thank you for being a Godly father. I remember you loving Mom. I remember you teaching me about Jesus. I remember you letting me win wrestling matches when I was young and not letting me win as I got older. I remember you letting me fail at things. I remember the spankings I got from you and Mom. I remember playing cards, foot races, and hockey with you. I remember you giving me my independence. I remember learning how to work from you. I'm sure I never thanked you enough for all the things you've done. God has different plans than ours right now and believe it or not, I'm okay with that. Judy and I don't need anyone's pity, we need their prayers." Dad and I stood there as I said a prayer. We hugged each other and finished chores.

I was slowly getting weaker and trimming was becoming quite a chore. I was able to get disability for financial help which allowed me to stop trimming feet. I started to visit kids in the hospital and sing at nursing homes. God spoke to me so much through those kids and adults. He taught me courage, honor, strength, and patience.

One day I ran into Dr. Baki in the hallway of the hospital. "Hey, Doc, how's it going?"

"Jude, I was going to call you today but the nurses said I would catch you here. I don't have a lot of time to explain, but there is a new treatment that you and Judy need to consider. A few days ago, I sent a letter your way explaining the details. The letter should be waiting for you when you get home. Please read it and call with any questions. Hey, and thanks for volunteering with the kids."

I have to admit, my curiosity was running rampant the rest of the day. I couldn't wait to get home and read his letter. I decided that Judy and I would read it together. Basically, the letter spoke of a new drug treatment that was on a trial basis and pretty hard on the body the first couple of days. It required two weeks in a hospital and one week in a nursing home. It sounded pretty good except for the nursing home part, but insurance wouldn't cover it any other way. My pride told me I was way too young to spend time in a nursing home. Judy and I prayed about it and decided to give it a try.

We were both optimistic as I entered the hospital. Our church family was praying for us and I was ready for anything that might help. The letter was right. The first couple days were miserable beyond belief. I felt like a rag doll with tubes sticking in and out of me in places I can't even mention. I was unable to talk with anyone since I had what felt like a garden hose down my throat. After the fourth day I was having second thoughts, wondering if we had made the right decision.

After two weeks I was moved to the nursing home and felt a little better. All I wanted to do was sleep. Judy was at my side pretty much the whole time. Mom or Mr. Olson would replace her when Judy needed a break. Harold, Perry and Wade came to visit me once, and I felt a little foolish laying there in bed incapacitated as my high school buddies stood over me.

"Jude, I've been praying for you," Harold said. "Is there anything I can get you?"

I could barely mumble, "Chocolate shake and Pete or Joe would be just fine."

The guys all laughed. They stood there and told stories of the good ol' days back in high school. They talked about hockey games, dances, rat hunting, and Mrs. Norman's class. It was great to hear them reminisce about days gone by. I dozed off while they talked, and then we heard her coming. It was Nurse Wagner heading our way.

"Gentlemen, I do believe you've stayed past your welcome. Now Mr. Bonner needs his sleep, so hit the road, boys." She spoke with all the eloquence of a drill sergeant!

The guys gave me one quick look as they were pushed out the door. I mumbled my goodbyes and tried to wave as they left. Nurse Wagner had quite the reputation in the nursing home. She did her job very well but was known for not making very many friends in the process. She had a running feud with one of the residents of the home, Mrs. Josephson, who was in her late eighties and roamed the halls with her walker. Unfortunately, Mrs. Josephson didn't have complete control of her bowels and she refused to wear protection, so she would leave deposits along the way that Mrs. Wagner would have to clean up. Nurse Wagner was in my room one day checking my vitals when she paused as she heard Mrs. Josephson clunking along with her walker down the hall.

"My, my, what should I do with that lady? She has caused me so much grief. To think that I have to follow her around. I have better things to do," Nurse Wagner complained.

"I think you should be thankful, ma'am."

My roommate, Mr. Torgerson, chuckled when I said that.

"Are you kidding? I always get the bad end of the stick. You just don't understand."

"You could be stuck cleaning up behind an elephant. And besides, remember Philippians: 'Do everything without complaining or arguing, so that you may become blameless and pure children of God without fault in a crooked and depraved generation.'"

Boy, that Bible verse lit a fire in her boiler room! She looked at me and stormed out of the room. My roommate laughed even louder. I thought, "How sad that God's word offends her so much." I soon caught a glimpse of her heading down the hall with a bucket and paper towels.

That night I didn't set any records on getting sleep. The medications I was taking were known for affecting sleep. The next morning I had a little breakfast and pretty much went right back to sleep with Judy at my side. As I dozed off, my mind went to dreaming about Fuzz, Herbie the bull, and Pete and Joe. In fact, my dream seemed so real I swear I could smell horse. Soon I was getting nuzzled by a big soft nose. Let me tell you, folks, some dreams do come true! I woke up and there stood Pete, big as a barn in my room at the nursing home. Mom, Perry, Mr. Olson and Harold had snuck Pete into my room. Pete had nuzzled me until I woke. I gave him a great big hug and he softly nickered as I held him.

"Pete, you big dumb horse, what are you doing in here? If Nurse Wagner catches you in here she'll send ya to the dog food factory. How did you guys get him in here without anyone seeing him?"

Judy stood there with the widest of grins on her face. "Well, we sent Harold over to the nurses' desk to sweet talk Nurse Wagner while Mr. Olson and Perry brought him in the side door. Notice he has his rubber boots on, and he's fresh off a nice bath," Judy explained.

Perry said, "Jude, what do you think? It was easier than we thought. Pete is so calm and easy going."

"Perry, keep in mind, you haven't got him out of here yet, but this is great! Oh, Pete, how is Joe doing?"

Pete went over and nosed around my roommate's bed and came back to stand by my bed. Mr. Torgerson didn't mind at all. He was a crude man in certain ways but we got along pretty well.

"Jude, we even brought a five-gallon pail just in case Pete needs to relieve himself while he's here," Perry said.

Right then my roommate, Mr. Torgerson, interrupted, "Jude my boy, keep in mind Nurse Battle Ax will be in here in a few minutes to check on both of us." In my state of mind I had forgotten about Nurse Wagner's morning check up. We were in a pickle and didn't have a lot of time to come up with a game plan. Pete didn't seem too worried, nor did Mr. Olson and Perry. They could hardly stop from busting a gut as they stood there.

"Okay, here's the plan," I said, "lead Pete over to Mr. Torgerson's side of the room and pull the curtain. When Nurse Battle Ax comes in, Mr. Torgerson will ask for some privacy and say that he needs to use the urinal. Perry, you stay with Pete as Mr. Olson, Judy and I visit with Nurse Wagner. Everybody in?"

I looked everyone in the eye and they all gave me the thumbs up. Even though Pete had a bath, horse smell still hung in the air. Judy gave the room a good spraying with air freshener. Perry led Pete over to the other side of the room and Mr. Olson closed the curtain behind them. It wasn't long before we heard footsteps in the hall heading our way. Sure enough, it was Nurse Wagner.

As she stepped into the room the smell stopped her in her tracks. I thought we were had! Harold stood right behind her in the doorway.

"Mr. Olson, don't you think you could have changed out of them barn clothes before you came to visit?" Mom asked at just the right time.

"Why certainly, why certainly."

Nurse Wagner shot a mean look over to Mr. Olson like he was

a hardened criminal. Mr. Olson did an excellent job keeping a straight face as she stared him down.

"Sorry, ma'am. I guess I need a few more manners or some clean clothes," Mr. Olson said as he looked back at her. "Why certainly."

Nurse Wagner checked me out and charted everything on the clipboard. Mr. Olson stood so she couldn't get too close to the curtain. Now came the real test. "Mr. Torgerson, may I come in and check you now?"

"By golly if you don't mind Nurse Ba... I mean Wagner, I would like a little privacy for the next few minutes."

"Are you okay this morning, Mr. Torgerson?"

"Ya know, Nurse Wagner, for some reason I feel strong as a horse this morning." Mr. Olson had just taken a sip of coffee right before Mr. Torgerson said that line and he blew it out twice as fast as it went in!

"Yes Nurse Wagner, I feel fine, but I do have some pretty bad gas and I need to use the urinal. Yes sir, a man's got to do what he's got to do at times, so if you'll just excuse me if it gets a little noisy over here and give me a little privacy." Just as Mr. Torgerson said the word "privacy," Pete let one rip. I looked at Judy and she looked back at me. Nurse Wagner's mouth hung open in dismay. "Sorry, ma'am, but by God I told the kitchen staff about serving green jello with apples in it! It gives a guy tremendous gas, and oh my, I've got to pee like a race horse!"

You guessed it! Pete started filling that five-gallon pail like there was no tomorrow. The room was dead silent except for what sounded like a high pressure hose filling a bucket. Nurse Wagner moved closer to the curtain to get a better listen. I noticed her shoes getting wet from the over spray. Needless to say, the aroma was beyond description. Mr. Olson and Perry were choking on their coffee and Judy and I could hardly contain ourselves.

"Nurse Wagner, by golly, please tell the kitchen about that jello!"

"Okay, Mr. Torgerson, are you done? Can I come in and check you now?"

"Oh no, Nurse Wagner. Excuse the French but you wouldn't want to see this horse's butt right now. Give me about an hour to settle down, please. Did you know that they make jello out of horse feet?"

"Thank you for that bit of trivia, Mr. Torgerson. I'll see you in an hour."

Harold watched Nurse Wagner walk down the hall to make sure she didn't double back. When he gave us the all clear, the room erupted with laughter. Every one of us was laughing so hard we were crying, even Mr. Torgerson. My stomach muscles were killing me, excuse the pun.

"Mr. Torgerson, that was a great performance. How did you think of all those lines to use?" I asked.

"Well, I didn't have much choice, so I figured I would have a little fun while I was at it."

Pete stood there like he owned the place as we talked about the good old days and retold the story of what just happened over and over. I'd never seen Mr. Torgerson smile and laugh so hard before that day.

It was soon time for Operation Escape, getting Pete back out of the place undetected. Harold went to smooth over Nurse Wagner again while Mr. Olson and Perry got ready to lead Pete down the hallway.

Sure enough, just before they led Pete out of the room, Mrs. Josephson strolled down the hallway. Harold noticed Nurse Wagner was watching every step Mrs. Josephson took, so he actually put his arm around her and led her to the coffee room. I gave Pete one last hug and off he went with Mr. Olson and Perry.

As I watched him lower his head to exit I saw his tail raising. Sure enough, Pete had to drop some road apples in the hallway. Judy said Mr. Olson and Perry hustled him out of there as Pete left several large deposits along the way. Mr. Torgerson and I were laughing as Judy came back in the room with a look of dismay on her face. "Jude, what am I going to do with that mess?"

All of a sudden, Harold stepped in the room laughing sheepishly. "I could only keep her contained for so long. She is all worried about cleaning up after Mrs. Josephson, so she went to get her cleaning supplies and will be here any second."

Judy asked Harold, "Did you see what Pete did in the hallway? What should I do?"

"Yes, ma'am, a blind man could see that mess. I think we should just lay low and let Nurse Wagner clean up after Mrs. Josephson."

Yes, sir, it wasn't long and we could hear Nurse Wagner mumbling to herself. It was all we could do to stop from laughing. Believe it or not, Harold had the audacity to step out in the hallway to see how it was going.

"Nasty, nasty. What a mess!" Harold declared. "Who, pray tell, is responsible for this handy work, Nurse Wagner?"

"Oh, that Josephson lady! All I do is clean up after her, but man, she's never dropped a load this big before. I swear she stores it up until my shift!"

"Ya know, maybe it's that green jello with apples in it. Yep, that sure is the mother load there. It's got to be that jello. Did you know they make jello out of horse's hooves?"

Judy was peeking out the door, taking it all in. With Harold's last comment, Nurse Wagner threw her towel in the bucket and just glared at him.

"Nurse Wagner, have you ever read Philippians?" Harold asked. I guess that was the last straw. She stood up and abruptly stormed down the hallway. "It was nice talking with you, ma'am. Have a nice day!"

It wasn't long and my stint in the nursing home was over. I said goodbye to Mr. Torgerson, Mrs. Josephson, and even Nurse Wagner. Judy baked some poppy seed muffins for all the staff. As Judy wheeled me down the hallway, all I could think of was getting home to my own bed. The sun blinded me as I was wheeled out the door. It was a beautiful October day and it felt so good to take in the crisp fall air. A red tailed hawk circled above us as we sat there.

We loaded up the van and headed home. Pete and Joe stood at the fence and whinnied as we pulled in. As I stepped out of the van, they trotted off with their tails as high as could be. They were happy to see me. Joe would bite at Pete's neck, and then Pete would spin and send a mock kick his way.

"Jude, do you want me to go with you to the fence?"

"No, I'll be fine." I slowly made my way over to the fence and held Pete in my left arm and Joe in my right. I gently blew in their noses and we talked as I looked them in the eye. They say a horse will never look you directly in the eye unless they're mean or they're going to die. Pete and Joe looked me directly in the eyes the whole time.

As I took a couple steps back toward the house a strange feeling come over me, as if someone was beside me. I looked each way and behind me. Nobody was there. Pete and Joe were still looking directly in my eyes. I took a few more steps and felt chills starting and the hair on the back of my neck rise. I slowly knelt down right there as God spoke with me.

"It's time, Jude."

"But God, I just took that new treatment!" I hesitantly said.

"Jude, it's time."

I sat there while my whole body blushed. Being in His presence was totally awesome. I was trembling as I was trying to understand. Judy came running out the door, crying all the way. She knelt down beside me and hugged me. I don't know how long we sat there as Judy wept and I silently praised our God.

In between the tears, Judy asked, "When is God taking you, Jude? What do I do without you?"

We sat there as I just held my lovely bride. What an honor to be married to such a woman. I leaned back and looked into Judy's eyes. "You have to make me some promises, Judy."

She looked away. "I can't do that, Jude, not in a time like this!"

"Remember, you can do all things through Him who gives you strength. Look me in the eyes, Judy. Promise me to stay strong, and that means not doubting God's plan. I'm not sure what to think Judy. I'm torn between Heaven and you."

I guess my timing wasn't the best. Judy screamed like I never heard a woman scream before and she pounded on my chest as hard as she could. Pete and Joe thundered around the pasture as she screamed at the top of her lungs. Gradually her screams subsided into tears again and I could feel her going limp. She soon crashed onto my lap like a rag doll. I wondered if she was going into shock. I carefully slipped my jacket off and wrapped her in it, and then decided I had to carry her into the house before we both froze. The cancer and the treatment had taken most of my strength, but I figured it was my last chance to carry my wife over the threshold.

I wiggled my way out from under her and squatted down beside her so I could lift with the most leverage. It was all I could do to get her even moving upward. I was trying to breathe right and keep my balance at the same time. Inch by inch I defied gravity. I finally got her up to my chest and started my slow way forward. I took one step, then another. The house seemed a mile away. I concentrated on the front door as I took each step.

Finally, Judy and I made it into the house. I laid her on the spare bed and covered her up. I checked her pulse and respirations and they seemed fine. Judy was just plain exhausted. I sat near her and started writing my wishes for pallbearers, songs, food, and maybe a role for Pete and Joe.

It was soon morning and Judy had slept that whole time, even as I did chores. She was just waking as I checked on her. "Honey, did you sleep well?"

Judy mumbled as she stretched and rubbed her eyes. "Ya know, Mrs. Bonner—" We were interrupted by a knock on the door. Who would be visiting at this time in the morning? I peeked out the door and there stood Mr. Olson.

"Jude, can I come in?"

"Yes, sir."

Mr. Olson stepped in the back entry and I could tell something was on his mind.

He stood there fussing with his hat in his hands without making much eye contact with me. Judy got up and started fixing breakfast for all of us. Soon we sat down at the table. Mr. Olson ate pretty well but my appetite was just not there.

As he wiped his mouth with his napkin, he started to talk. "Kids, what can I do for you? Do you need any money or groceries? Is there work that needs to be done around here?"

I answered back, "Mr. Olson, we're fine right now, but you'll be the first one we call when we need help."

He spoke cautiously as he wiped his brow of sweat. "Jude, remember when we talked about you doing my funeral years back?"

"Yes sir. It was when you bought the hitch wagon."

He looked off in the distance. "I hope I'm wrong, but you might be needing that wagon before me. And if so, I'd be honored to let you use the wagon and the harness. I could hook Pete and Joe if that's what you want."

Judy got up and stood behind me with her hands on my shoulders. You could tell she was having a hard time with this discussion.

"Mr. Olson, if I remember correctly, that was the agreement back then."

"Yes, yes it was."

"In fact, I was just putting some plans together last night related to this very subject."

"Jude, I'm so sorry." He teared up some and got up and looked out the window. "You are like a son to me and I thank you for that. I remember when you were a snotty-nosed little kid, catching frogs, trapping gophers, shooting sparrows along with a few of my barn windows. All those things that a boy needs to do. Now look at ya, you're a man fighting a man's battle. I wish I could do something more for you. I've prayed to God almighty to allow me to trade places."

"How 'bout hitching Pete and Joe and going for a ride with me on Sunday?"

"Why certainly, why certainly. I'd like to do that for you. Now I need to leave this envelope for you two. This is a gift from me to you so don't hurt my feelings by not accepting it. Use it as you wish and let me know if you need more. See ya this Sunday afternoon."

He stood up, placed the envelope on the table, and walked out the door. Judy was silent as I reached for the white envelope. Inside it were twenty brand new one hundred dollar bills. God bless Mr. Olson.

When Judy and I got home from church on Sunday. Mr. Olson had the geldings hitched. Mom, Dad and Becky's family came too. I noticed my body couldn't take the jarring of the ride and I couldn't roughhouse with my nephews like before. Yes, my illness was making an old man out of my body. Many times Judy would ask the question of why I had to go when I was still so young. I decided to prove to Judy it's all in perspective.

As we sat there resting the geldings, I asked my four-year-old nephew Conway, "Do you think I'm old, Conway?"

"You betcha! Uncle Jude, you're super old."

I grabbed him and gave him a big bear squeeze. I looked at Judy and she had a tear running down her cheek. Mom did, too.

By the time we got back home I was very stiff and Dad had to help me down. I slowly made my way back to the house as Dad and Mr. Olson unhitched Pete and Joe. I felt bad leaving them, but I had no strength left.

For the next couple of weeks I had good days and bad. One day I would feel fine, the next I was weak as a baby. Judy and I moved my stuff downstairs in the spare bedroom along with a hospital bed. Judy and I sat together in the evenings and finished planning the funeral. We decided to have the youth group be pallbearers. I made sure Judy understood that they were to do their job. In other words, I didn't want the funeral home guys touching the casket. Harold and the youth group were going to sing and Pete and Joe would haul me to my final resting place with the pallbearers following behind.

It was time to say goodbye to the youth group. I was getting too weak to put any energy into that. Judy and Mom fixed a bunch of treats and had a few games lined up. I sat there as the kids played, hollered, and stuffed their faces. I thought long and hard on what type of talk they should hear from me for the last time. "Hey, guys, it's devotion time. Gather' round." I said a quick prayer and dove into my talk.

"This is your last meeting with me. Next week you'll have a new part-time youth pastor. You need to realize this new guy is not as good-looking or athletic as me, but you will like him. God has plans for me right now that only He understands. I've lived a full life and had many great times with this group of kids. I remember wrestling with the guys, singing with the girls, and pitting guys against girls in games and trivia questions. But most of all, I remember how God has worked in the lives of you kids. It wasn't Jude Bonner, it was God. So with that said, God will bring another person into your lives to fill this role."

I stopped to catch my breath for a moment. "The best part of all is I was able to witness many of you come to Christ. What an honor! I'm going to miss you kids, and when I'm gone don't forget about Judy. Please call her and check on her every once in a while." I took a small sip of water. "My last request would be to use your muscles. I would be honored if you would be my pallbearers."

I think they thought I was kidding. They sat there not saying anything. I looked at a few of my older kids for an answer. I finally got some nods of approval from several older kids.

After my little talk, each kid stood in line and I said goodbye to each one individually. It was a long night and I was very tired when I got home.

Each day I would try to get out of the house to see the geldings. Winter was setting in so some of those cold days were pretty rough. I was no longer strong enough to lift bales of hay, so Judy was doing that for me. I truly believe my body was that of an eighty-year-old man. I fell down a couple times outside and could barely get back up, which I never told Judy. It still amazed me how God was with me every day. I didn't fear dying, I wasn't in that much pain, and so far I didn't need diapers.

Chapter 18
"The End"

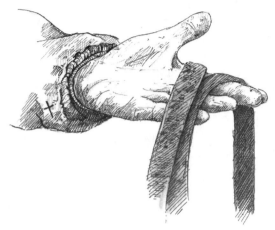

It was after the new year when Jude required hospice care. He was just too much for me to handle. There were several nurses that came in shifts. He was bedridden and didn't talk much anymore. One evening, I set up a candlelit dinner for the two of us. Mom Bonner came in and cooked his favorite meal from when he was a kid. He only ate about two bites. When we were done eating, I played piano for my Jude as he lay there motionless. After that, I lay down beside him and held him. Jude was leaving me and oh, how I wanted to hold him and make things better.

"Judy," Jude whispered, "did you know I'm married to the prettiest girl in the world? Thank you for the music. I will miss you and thank you for being my wife and my best friend. Remember the day I carried you out of the road ditch?" He hesitated as he struggled to breathe, then continued. "I remember the day..." Jude lay there catching his breath as I wiped tears away. "Judy, I'm so tired." He slowly turned his head my way. "Do you know I love you?"

I buried my head into his chest and wept like a baby. "Jude, I love you so much, what am I going to do without you." I wiped tears from my face and kissed his forehead. "Thank you for being my friend. I love Jude Bonner." I wasn't supposed to sleep with him, but I did that night. I really don't think I slept at all, but I'm so glad I spent that night beside him. That was the last time Jude spoke to anyone.

The next day Dr. Baki came to check on Jude. He checked Jude's pulse and respirations and called me out to the kitchen. "Judy, Jude probably has a couple of days at best. He will be in a lot of pain so I have left extra morphine for the hospice nurse. Anyone that needs to say goodbye should do it soon. That should be immediate family only. And Judy, make sure you spend time with him, read to him, and hold his hands. Any questions?"

Mom Bonner had moved in with us to be with her son. She read to him many hours, mostly out of God's word. I was dozing on and off as Mom Bonner was sitting on the side of the bed with Jude saying her goodbye.

"Jude, this is your mother, I hope you can hear me. I want you to know that you are so going to be missed. I love you so much. Dad and I will watch over Judy for you. I can't believe this is for real, Jude. You are my first child, and now I have to bu---." She fell to her knees at the side of the bed. With time she regained her composure.

"Jude, we never had that little talk about how many cookies you stole over the years for you and Fuzz, or why I never had ice cream in the freezer. Do you realize how many times I had to clean your room back in the day, give you a spit bath on the way to church, or hold you at gunpoint to change your undies? Maybe you and Jesus will have those discussions. Thank you for all the good times, Jude. Oh, how I love you." She was still kneeling by his bed when she looked up to the heavens.

"Jude, it's okay if you need to go. Don't hold on any longer. You're in God's hands now. God Bless my son, Jude Wayne Bonner. Goodbye." She kissed him on his lips.

I had to leave the room after that goodbye. I felt sick to my stomach. Maybe that is why Jude and I never had kids. I'd never have to go through this with my own kids. Through my blurred eyes I looked out the kitchen window and there sat a bright red cardinal on a limb of our flowering crab tree. Jude and I had tried for years to get cardinals and now I was looking at one. What gives?

Except for going to the bathroom, I spent every second at Jude's side. We had his close family come in and say goodbye. Jude was basically in a coma at this time and he looked pretty bad with all the weight loss, dark circles under his eyes, sunken cheeks, and the smell of cancer in the air. Many people were praying for us, and I could feel God's presence in the room.

It was the tenth of January and thirty below zero outside when Jude went home to be with the Lord. His Mom and Dad were there along with Mr. Olson. He took a couple large breaths and arched his back, then he slowly curled into the fetal position and was gone.

As soon as he was gone, Pete and Joe went crazy in the pasture. They whinnied like I'd never heard them before. They ran back and forth along the fence as they looked toward the house, pawing the ground. They knew their Jude was gone.

I sat there and held his hand until it got cool to the touch. My Jude was gone. I eventually got to the phone to call the coroner and the funeral home. As we waited for them to show, Jude's dad spoke. "If it is all right with you, Judy, I would like to carry him out to the hearse."

I couldn't speak so I just nodded. The coroner checked Jude over closely and gave the hospice nurse the okay to pull the IVs. When they were done, I needed to change him one last time. I asked everyone to leave, pulled his diaper off, and replaced it with a pair of undies. My Jude was not going to the funeral home in a diaper!

Oh, the sight of that hearse pulling in the drive. Dad Bonner asked them to get the gurney out and place it right behind the hearse. He came back in and asked if it was okay to take my Jude. I bent over and kissed his cool stiff lips one last time. Dad Bonner cradled Jude in his arms and carried him out of the house as I followed them. He gently laid his body on the gurney. Pete and Joe were completely silent as they looked on. I collapsed as they pulled a sheet over his head. Dad and Mom Bonner helped me up as Jude was loaded into the back of the hearse. I couldn't understand what was really happening. We watched as the hearse slowly pulled out of the driveway. Pete and Joe were screaming at the top of their lungs as the hearse left.

What I hadn't thought of was how empty the house would feel that first night. I barely slept and when I did, I had crazy dreams and would wake in a cold sweat. As I lay there I asked myself what I would do with his clothes and belongings. I'm not sure if I would ever have the courage to go through his closet.

Mom Bonner called me the next morning and said that Harold, Perry and Wade were digging the grave for Jude by hand through all the frost. The next questions she asked really took me by surprise. "Judy, I'd like your permission to dress Jude and do his hair. In fact you might consider going with me. The mortuary needs to know by noon today if we are going to dress him. Think about it and give me a call. God bless." I was stunned. I'd never thought about doing that part for Jude. My mind just raced. What would Jude like? Could I really do it? Would he be all stiff? What would he feel like?

"Lord, I need to talk. I have mixed emotions about this clothes thing. I'm scared and lonely and not sure if this is right for me, Lord. Please give me an answer, Lord. Amen."

As soon as I said, "Amen," the phone started ringing again. "Hello?"

"Judy, it's your mother. I hope you got some sleep last night. Your dad and I talked it over and we would like to buy you a new dress for Jude's funeral. I could pick you up before lunch if you wish."

"Mom, I haven't even thought about what to wear yet. I don't think there are a lot of options in my closet, so maybe we should do that."

"How about I pick you up in time to take you out to lunch, then we find that new dress? I promise we can make short work of this because I know you're tired. See ya in a bit, bye."

I called Mom Bonner back and gave her permission to dress Jude and told her I had to get a new dress and shoes.

Mr. Olson came over for Pete and Joe to get them ready for the big day. I stood and watched from the front window. First they wouldn't let Mr. Olson catch them. When he finally did catch them, they looked like they were trying to bite and kick at him. Mr. Olson did a lot of talking with them and he gradually got them loaded. I'd never seen them act like that before.

Mom and I found a dress that was appropriate and had a good talk. When she dropped me off back home the place seemed extra barren without the geldings. The next day was the wake. Mom, Dad and the Bonners went early with me to view the body for the first time. I held onto Dad's arm as we walked into the room where Jude was. I was scared to look at first. Jude had looked pretty rough at the end and I was afraid he would still look bad. I gradually pulled my eyes toward his face as I squeezed Dad's arm as hard as I could. There my Jude lay, and he looked like he did the day we got married. Thank you, Lord! The room was silent as I studied every one of Jude's features: his eyes, his face, his lips, his hair, his hands, his clothes, his eye brows, his chin. He was beautiful. I reached out and touched his face and brushed his hair with my fingers. Deep down I think I was checking if this was real. Was Jude really dead? I think I stood with Jude for an hour without moving as the Bonners and Mom and Dad held me. As I was crying my eyes out, I spoke with Jude, "Harold, Perry and Wade are digging through the frost by hand for your grave, and Mr. Olson came over and picked up Pete and Joe. He promised he would have them at their best for your last ride. I wish you could see me in my new dress. I think you would like it. Jude, do you know how nice you look today?" Next thing I knew, Mom Bonner was talking to me.

"Honey, they have to move Jude into the main room now. The people will be coming in about an hour. Do you need anything to eat or drink before they get here?"

I shook my head no. I used the restroom and went right back to Jude's side. I dreaded the thought of him being alone. The funeral director suggested we come up with a game plan on where we would stand and how the flow of people would travel.

I decided to suggest how we would stand. "I want to be as close to Jude as possible. This will be the last time we can be a couple. I would like to have the Bonners stand to my left and greet visitors before they get to the casket. And Mom, Dad, how about you guys stand to the right of me and greet them after they spend time with Jude and I?"

The next people to come were Becky, Wade, and their kids Nancy, Jeff, and Troy. Wade was basically carrying Becky the closer they got to the casket. I knelt down and Nancy ran into my arms.

"Aunt Judy, why is mommy crying so much? She cried all the way here, Aunt Judy. Dad said Uncle Jude was hurt real bad. Tell me, Aunt Judy." I lifted Nancy up, carried her to a chair at the side, and sat her on my lap.

Nancy and I sat there in silence as Becky hung onto the edge of the casket with Mom and Dad Bonner holding Jeff and Troy. Becky was totally losing it, and rightfully so; Jude and her were very close. I held Nancy with tears streaming down my face as I watched Becky struggle.

"See, Aunt Judy, is mommy okay?"

"Oh Nancy, if you could only understand. I'm so sorry."

"Is Uncle Jude sleeping? When will he wake up?"

"Nancy, Uncle Jude has gone to heaven, so you will only see

him there someday."

"What do you mean? I thought only dead people went to heaven, Aunt Judy."

"Nancy." I looked right into her little blues eyes. "Jude is dead, Nancy."

She looked away and started to cry. "Can I go be with Mom, Aunt Judy?"

I released my grip and Nancy slid off my lap and ran toward Becky. I followed silently behind and stood. Becky lifted Nancy up and held her as they stood over the open casket. Nancy just stared at Jude, not really knowing what to think.

"Mommy, can I touch him?" Becky looked back at me. I gave her the okay. Nancy reached out and held the back of her hand against his cold cheek. "Why is he so cold, Mommy?"

Wade stepped in as Becky was losing it again and grabbed Nancy. Mr. Bonner put Jeff down and held Becky at the side of the casket. Jeff came over to me and I picked him up and gave him a huge hug.

"Aunt Judy, why are your eyes so red? Is it because Uncle Jude is hurt real bad?"

"Yes, Jeff, yes."

"Dad said if I was bigger I could help carry Jude. I'm sorry I'm not bigger." He started to tear up a little. "Can I give Jude my favorite tractor, Aunt Judy? Dad said I could do that instead of helping carry Uncle Jude."

I lost it. I buried my face into his little neck and just wept as I held him tight. I slowly lowered him to the ground and held his cheeks so to look him in the eye. "Jeff, I think Uncle Jude would love your favorite tractor. You know something, Jeff?"

"What?"

"I love you!" I gave him a kiss on his little forehead.

Jeff trotted over to Becky and she lifted him up so he could put the tractor alongside Jude. I gradually made my way over and stood with Becky in silence as we held hands.

Becky softly spoke between sobs. "Judy, I'm so sorry. He was the best brother in the world. Why, why, why? I'm supposed to help you be strong and here I am crying like a fool. I'm so sorry, Judy."

I held her into my shoulder and we just stood there some more. "Becky, Jude loved you and your kids so much. He's going to miss them so much. Can you help me, Becky?" She pulled away and looked at me. "I'm not sure how to get through tonight on my own. Will you stand beside me?"

Becky broke down again right after I asked her for help. Wade came over and helped her to the bathroom. Ten minutes later Becky was standing beside me with a box of tissues.

It wasn't long and the people were there. Jude and I greeted people for four hours straight. It was very tiring, but I had to do it for Jude's sake. Many people say strange things to you and it was hard to reply back at times. It was great to talk face-to-face with people whom Jude had talked of over the years but I never had met. What I wasn't prepared for was leaving Jude that night. It really bothered me that Jude would be in that building all by himself. It's like I was walking out on him. Dad and Mr. Bonner practically carried me out. I did not sleep at all that night.

I do think God was on our side the day of the funeral. It was thirty above zero, sunny, and no wind. Pete and Joe were looking pretty sharp. Mr. Olson had their manes and tails all curried out. But they weren't themselves that day. They would prance around and not stand still. Their heads were way up in the air and they seemed not to pay a lot of attention to Mr. Olson. You could hear Mr. Olson calmly talking to them. "Easy boys, easy. I know ya miss him but we need to do this right. He'll be here pretty quick, boys. Settle down now, settle down."

The church was full that day. Many people I hadn't seen since our wedding, like Mrs. Norman, Carl Toney, Doc Strand, and many of our high school classmates were there. We allowed time for anyone who wanted to say something about Jude to stand and speak into a microphone. Wow, it was very humbling! I had been married to Jude for eight years, and I didn't truly understand how God worked through him. During this time there were many laughs and many tears.

The bright light of the sun came in as the back church door opened. In stepped Greg Shants in an orange jump suit followed by a deputy sheriff. The place fell dead silent as Greg slowly made his way to Jude's casket in the front of the church. He placed both of his shackled hands on Jude's casket and wept uncontrollably for several minutes. Greg slowly turned and faced the crowd. "I was Jude Bonner's worst enemy in high school. My mission was to make his life miserable, and I was good at it. Now I stand in front of his casket begging for your forgiveness." He wiped his eyes and looked back at the casket. "There is one secret

Jude kept even from Judy, and that was his visits to me in prison. God used Jude to help lead me to Christ's saving grace. Jude was a Godly man and I will truly miss him. I thank the Lord for Jude Bonner." Greg walked to the back of the church as the ushers were literally passing boxes of tissues down the aisles. Harold and the youth group went up, surrounded his casket, and sang their songs.

After the songs, Kelly slowly made her way to the front of the church and gave the casket a big hug and kiss. She turned to address the dead quiet congregation. "Mr. Bonna was friend to me. He let me ride Pete. I loved Mr. Bonna. When I was younger I was gonna marry Mr. Bonna. He told me I special. I love Mr. Bonna." She walked over to me and gave me a great big hug as tears poured down her face.

Row by row we filed out of the church to create a corridor for the pallbearers to carry Jude to the hitch wagon. The youth group kids took turns on the casket, girls included. As the casket came closer to Pete and Joe, I watched them to see how they would respond. The pallbearers stopped crossways with the casket right in front of the geldings. Pete and Joe slowly lowered their massive heads between pallbearers and nuzzled the casket with their soft lips. They each softly whinnied and pawed at the ground with their front feet and then continued to nuzzle Jude's casket. The moisture from their nostrils left the top of the casket a little frosty. As the casket was taken away they stood at attention, looking straight forward, heads high, not moving a muscle. Their coats were gleaming, along with the patent leather harness and the sun against the white snow.

Soon the casket was at the back of the wagon. A couple of youth group kids lowered the tailgate and they proceeded to lift the casket into place. Hitch wagons are pretty high off the ground, so the kids had a little struggle getting it up there. A few men jumped in from the sides and gave them an extra lift. After Jude was in place, Mr. Olson and Jude's Dad lifted me in with Jude. As I held him, I realized that this was it. I would never hold him again. I would never in this world see him again. I would never cook for him again. I would never wash his clothes again. I would never hear him clang his spoon on his cereal bowl again. I would never have to clean his whiskers out of the bathroom sink again. I would never feel his warmth as we slept. I would never feel his touch. I would never look him in the eye again. This just seemed impossible, and I silently pleaded with God to open his casket and let us live happily ever after.

In the background I eventually heard Mr. Olson's voice. "Pete, Joe, get up." I waited to feel the wagon move, but we were still. "Pete, Joe, get up," Mr. Olson repeated. Again we didn't move. Pete and Joe were not moving on command. Soon Dad Bonner grabbed their bridles and tried to encourage them to step out while Mr. Olson spoke to them, but that just seemed to make things worse. Pete and Joe actually had their front feet off the ground a couple times as they refused to move forward.

Mr. Olson asked Dad Bonner to come up there. They talked back and forth a little and soon they both came down. Next thing I knew we were moving without a driver! Once Jude was loaded in the back, Pete and Joe took that as him driving them. They were not going to move till that driver's seat was empty! What a sight! Pete and Joe were right in step, slowly prancing in total unison. Mr. Olson walked ahead of them while the others walked behind the wagon. They did turns perfectly, their pace was steady, and they stayed in step the whole way. They were on a mission: their eyes full of determination, nostrils flaring as they spewed steam, necks arched, ears pointing straight ahead, heads as high as ever, hooves pounding the pavement like a drum beat, and all this with no driver. Pete and Joe didn't miss a beat as they covered the mile out to the cemetery.

Mr. Olson stopped them at the entrance and let everyone go past to form a corridor to the grave site. Dad and Dad Bonner helped me get out, and we walked though the corridor of people to the open grave. It was remarkable. The crowd was silent, and all eyes were on Pete and Joe in the distance. Soon Mr. Olson walked toward the rest of us. The geldings stood there like statues on the pure white snow surrounded by the bright blue sky, watching every move Mr. Olson made as he quietly walked down the corridor and stood where Pete and Joe would stop. He looked my way and gave me a small nod. I looked back at Pete, Joe and Jude. How I wanted to have them stand there forever. I actually caught myself thinking that maybe if I kept them there, I wouldn't have to place Jude in the ground. As I stood there thinking, a thistle seed caught my attention as it floated by. I watched it till it was out of sight. I looked back toward the geldings and pursed my lips, and whistled like Jude.

Sure enough, Pete and Joe whinnied and exploded into a full

high stepping trot heading right down the corridor of people. I'd never seen them glide across the ground like they did that day. They were completely focused on the task at hand, which was to bring Jude's body to its final resting place. The corridor of people broke into applause as Pete and Joe thundered past them, which seemed to excite Pete and Joe all the more. The geldings were locked in on Mr. Olson and heading his way like a finely-tuned freight train. People behind Mr. Olson were starting to get nervous and were moving away. The geldings were getting closer and showing no signs of slowing down. Mr. Olson stood there firmly and looked them right in the eyes. Twenty feet away, fifteen feet away, ten feet away, five feet away! Without a word, Pete and Joe put the brakes on and skidded to a stop six inches from Mr. Olson. The crowd stopped applauding to wipe away tears as Pete and Joe stood at full attention. The only thing to be heard was the sound of Pete and Joe's heavy breathing. Every once in a while you could smell warm horse, exactly what Jude would have wanted.

The tailgate was opened and the kids carefully took out the casket. Soon Jude was on the frame work above the hole. Everyone crowded in as tightly as they could. I squeezed Dad's hand for all I was worth. The minister spoke the normal burial verses and we sang, "It is well with my soul." I don't believe there was a dry eye in the bunch. As they sang, I mustered up the strength to stand and placed my hands on the casket. I silently said my final goodbye to the man I loved.

After the song Harold, Perry, Becky, Wade, Mr. Olson, Mom and Dad Bonner, Kelly and even Greg lowered Jude into the ground. As the crowd dispersed, I stood by the geldings as we watched the guys shovel the dirt back in the hole. Pete and Joe were softly snorting in my ears. I had so many things running through my mind. How would I be able to leave this cemetery? How many times would I come back? Was this for real? What were Pete and Joe thinking?

As I looked up into their big dark eyes, they each had tears running down their cheeks.

About Pete and Joe

Ever since the release of *Jude's Gentle Giants*, Pete and Joe have become local celebrities. They have been on WCCO-TV's *Life to the Max*, and a *Rural Heritage* segment on RFD-TV. They have gone to numerous book signings with me and have met many young adults who can't wait to get a picture taken with them. With all the limelight, Pete and Joe are still themselves!

Pete was born on March 20th and Joe on March 13th of 2006 on the Art Eller farm near Pierz, Minnesota. Their first six months were spent with their moms and other mares and colts in a beautiful pasture with a fresh water stream running through it. Pete and Joe are half – brothers, with the same sire.

In August of 2006, Les Graham came to inspect Pete and Joe. After Pete and Joe were weaned off their mothers in September of 2006, they were bought by Les Graham of New London, Minnesota and were loaded into a horse trailer for the 80 mile ride home. At home, Pete and Joe shared a pasture with Ladd, a 21 year old Percheron gelding. They did their best to make Ladd's life miserable with their playful antics.

Training started a couple weeks after Pete and Joe were settled in their new home. Pete was fairly easy to train and learned quickly. Joe had his own ideas, so Les spent double the time in training Joe. Training involved learning to lead, feet work, sacking out, backing, honoring a human's space, and eventually hitching with Ladd for pulling. Pete and Joe tried to run away the first couple of times of being hitched, but Ladd kept them in line. Pete and Joe do sleigh rides, cutting and raking hay, some funerals, weddings, and a few parades.

Both Pete and Joe grew up to be around 2100 pounds and close to 18 hands high. Both horses are black with very uncharacteristic white blazes on their faces. Pete has a wide white blaze and a little white on both back feet, while Joe has a narrow white blaze and a little white on one back foot. Pete is as steady as a rock when hitched or ridden and has a very smooth trot. Joe is not as trustworthy as Pete when hitched and requires an experienced driver to keep him in line. Pete loves to be scratched and curried and Joe loves to put his muzzle in your face so you can blow air into his nostrils.

Did You Find the Cross?

Mike Bregel the illustrator has drawn a cross into each illustration. Some are fairly obvious, others are somewhat hidden. Did you see them the first time or do you need to go back and find them?

I again thank you for taking time to read my lastest novel, *Surrendering the Reins*.

To have a captive audience is both an honor and a big responsibility. I pray that I have not dishonored God with my words.

Speaking of God. It is my hope that my books may have brought you closer with Jesus Christ, or maybe even taught you that ANYONE can have a personal relationship with our Lord and Savior Jesus Christ.

Romans 10:9-10 "That if you confess with your mouth, 'Jesus is Lord,' and believe in your heart that God raised Him from the dead, you will be saved. For it is with your heart that you believe and are justified, and it is with your mouth that you confess and are saved."

About the Illustrator

Mike Bregel was born in 1987 in the frozen tundra of Willmar, Minnesota. He studied graphic design at the University of Minnesota Duluth. He has shown work at the Tweed Museum of Art and won the Howard W. Lyons/ Alice Tweed Tuohy Award at the U of M Duluth Annual Juried Student Show. Since then Mike has been on a creative roller coaster that has included freelance illustration, commissioned paintings and professional web & print design. He co-owns and designs for Horizon Clothing Company and currently works as a creative marketing specialist at Life-Science Innovations.

You can find more of his work at bregelart.com